# Contents

# Off for the Holidays

One morning, at the beginning of the summer holidays, four children sat in an express train, feeling tremendously excited.

'Now we're really off!' said Mike. 'My word – think of it – two months in a little house by the sea! Bathing, paddling, fishing, boating – what fun we shall have!'

'All the same, I wish Mummy and Daddy were coming with us,' said Nora, Mike's twin sister. 'I shall miss them – especially after being away at school all term, and only seeing them once.'

'Well, they couldn't take the whole lot of us with them on their lecture tour!' said Peggy sensibly. 'They will join us at Spiggy Holes as soon as they can.'

'Spiggy Holes! Doesn't that sound an exciting name for a holiday place?' said Jack. 'Spiggy Holes – I wonder why it's called that. I suppose there are holes or caves or something.'

The four children had come home from school the day before. Nora and Peggy had arrived back from their girls' school, and Mike and Jack from their boys' school. They had spent the night at home with their father and mother, and now they were off, all alone, to Spiggy Holes.

Jack was the most excited of the four, for he had never

been to the sea before! He was not really the brother of Mike, Nora, and Peggy, and had no father and mother of his own.

But the children's parents had taken him for their own child, because he had helped Mike, Peggy, and Nora so much when they had run away from an unkind aunt and uncle. Captain Arnold, the children's father, had left them at a farm with his sister, whilst he and his wife had tried to fly to Australia in a tiny aeroplane.

Captain and Mrs Arnold had been lost for months on a desert island, and when it seemed as if they would never come back, the children's aunt treated them unkindly. They had made friends with Jack, who had helped them to run away to a secret island in a lake, and there the children had lived together until they had heard that their parents had been found and had come back to England to look for them.

As Jack had no people of his own, and was very fond of Mike, Nora and Peggy, Captain and Mrs Arnold had said that he should live with them just as if he were another of their children – and Jack had been very happy.

He had gone to boarding school with Mike, and now here they all were together again for the summer holidays. At first they had been sad to hear that Captain and Mrs Arnold were to go to Ireland to lecture there all about their flying adventures – but now that they were on their way to Cornwall together, to live in a house on the cliffs, and do just what they liked, the children couldn't help feeling excited and happy.

'Who's going to look after us at Spiggy Holes?' asked Jack.

'Somebody called Miss Dimity,' said Nora. 'I don't know anything about her except that Mummy says she is nice.'

'Miss Dimity!' said Peggy. 'She sounds sort of timid and mouse-like. I shall call her Dimmy.'

The others laughed. 'You wait till you see what she's like!' said Mike. 'She might be tall and strict and have a loud voice.'

The train roared on and on. Jack looked at a map on the wall. 'I say' he said. 'It looks as if Spiggy Holes isn't so very far from our secret island! I wonder if we could go over and see it. Dear little secret island – 1 expect it's looking grand now.'

'It's a good distance,' said Mike, looking at the map. 'About forty miles, I should think. Well, we'll see. I'd just love to see our secret island again.'

'Let's have our lunch now,' said Peggy, undoing the luncheon basket. 'Look what Mummy's given us!'

There were chicken sandwiches, tomato sandwiches, biscuits of all kinds, lemonade to drink, and apples and bananas.

'Jolly good,' said Mike, taking his share of the lunch. 'Mummy's great. She always knows what we like!'

'How long is it before we get to Spiggy Holes?' asked Nora, eating her chicken sandwiches hungrily.

'We get to the nearest station at half-past four this afternoon,' said Mike. 'But that's six miles from Spiggy Holes. There's to be a car or something to meet us.'

The time passed rather slowly. They had their books to read, and they played games of counting the signal-boxes and tunnels – but long before half-past four came they all felt tired, dirty, and hot.

7

'I'm going to sleep,' said Nora, and she put her feet up on the seat.

'Sleep!' said Mike scornfully. 'I couldn't possibly go to sleep now.'

All the same, he was fast asleep in a few minutes! So were they all, whilst the train thundered along through the sunny countryside, rushing under bridges, past stations and through tunnels at a tremendous speed.

The children only awoke as the train was slowing down in a station. Mike leapt up and looked out of the window.

'I say! Our station is the next one!' he yelled to the others. 'Wake up, you sleepy-heads, wake up! Get your things down from the rack, and make yourselves a bit tidy. You look dreadful.'

So they all cleaned themselves up, and got down their things. They were just ready when the train slowed up again and it was time to get out.

They jumped out, one after the other. Mike called to a porter, 'We've two trunks in the van. Will you get them out, please?'

The porter ran to do so. Jack wandered out into the

8

yard to see if any car had come to meet them. But there was none. Only a sleepy brown horse stood there, with a farm wagon behind him. A farm lad stood at his head.

'Are you Master Arnold?' he said to Jack. 'I'm meeting a party of four children to take them to Spiggy Holes.'

'Good,' said Jack. He called to the others. 'Hey, Mike! Nora! Peggy! There's a wagonette here to take us all. Hurry!'

The porter wheeled out the two trunks. The children piled themselves and their belongings into the wagonette and grinned at the farm lad, who looked a jolly sort of fellow. He got up into the driving-seat, cracked his whip and off they went trundling over the six miles to Spiggy Holes.

It was wonderful country that they passed through. The sea lay on one side, far down the cliff, as blue as the sky above. The cliffs were magnificent, and the coast was very rocky. Here and there the sea splashed around enormous rocks, and washed them with white spray.

On the other side were fields and hills. Poppies blazed by the roadside, and blue chicory flowers shone as brightly as the sky. The children were thrilled with everything.

'Hope the weather keeps on being sunny and warm like this,' said Mike. 'I shall live in a swimsuit!'

'So shall I,' said the others at once.

The horse trotted on. The children could hear the sound of the waves breaking on the shore far below. They were driving along a high, winding cliff road, and the sea wind blew hard in their faces. It was a very pleasant breeze, for the sun was hot, and still high in the sky.

'What's our house called?' Mike asked the farm lad, who was driving.

'It's called Peep-Hole,' said the lad.

'Peep-Hole!' said Jack, surprised. 'What an odd name!'

'You'll be seeing it in a minute,' said the lad. 'There it be!'

He pointed with his whip – and the four children saw the odd little house that was to be their home and the centre of their strange adventures for the next few weeks.

It was a funny crooked house, with a strange little tower built on one side of it. It was set in a hollow in the cliffs, and was turned towards the sea.

'It's called Peep-Hole because it really is a kind of peep-hole out to sea, set in the middle of those two cliffs,' said the farm lad. 'And from the tower you can see the tower of the old house set back on the cliff behind those tall trees there. They do say that in smugglers' days someone in the Peep-Hole used to flash signals to someone watching in the tower of the Old House.'

'I say! This sounds exciting,' said Jack. 'Smugglers – and towers – and flashing lights – and I suppose there are caves too.'

'Scores of them,' said the lad, grinning. 'You mind you don't get lost in some of them, or get caught by the tide. This is a rare dangerous coast for children.'

'Here's the Peep-Hole,' cried Nora, as they drew up outside the funny house with its one tall tower. 'And look – that must be Miss Dimity at the door! And she's just as mouse-like as you said, Peggy!'

All the children looked at Miss Dimity. She was a small, oldish woman, with neat grey hair, a little smiling face, and big grey eyes that looked timid and kind.

'Welcome to the Peep-Hole, children!' she cried in a little bird-like voice.

'Thank you, Miss Dimity!' said the children, and they each shook hands politely.

'I hope you'll have a good time here,' said Miss Dimity, leading the way indoors. 'Your rooms are in the tower. I thought you would like that.'

'In the tower!' cried Nora, with a squeal that made Miss Dimity jump. 'Oh, how lovely, lovely, lovely!'

Miss Dimity led the way to a funny little spiral staircase that went up and up and round and round to the top of the tower. In the tower were two rooms, one above the other. They were not very large and were perfectly round.

'Now you can wash and brush your hair and then come down to tea,' said Miss Dimity, in her firm, gentle voice. And she added again, 'I do hope you will have a good time here.'

She didn't guess what a *strange* time the children would have – poor Miss Dimity!

11

# At Spiggy Holes

The children washed and tidied themselves. They chattered loudly all the time. The boys had the top room, and as it had four windows, one on each side of the round tower, they had four different views.

'This window looks over the sea for a long way,' said Jack, peering out. 'And the next one looks on the cliffs – and this one looks overland and has a jolly good view of that old house up there – and this one just looks over the roofs of Peep-Hole.'

'That old house looks rather interesting and mysterious,' said Mike. 'It's very big. I wonder who lives there.'

'Come along, children!' called Miss Dimity. 'Tea is ready.'

They all ran downstairs, laughing at the quaint little winding staircase. They felt so happy. It was such fun to be all together again, after three months at school – it was nice to think of the lovely long weeks stretching before them, full of sunshine and fun.

There was a splendid tea, with three kinds of home-made cakes, and some delicious honey made by Miss Dimity's own bees. There was no tea to drink – just big mugs of cold creamy milk.

Miss Dimity sat at the head of the table, and asked

them about their journey down. The children liked her. She laughed at their jokes, and didn't seem to mind how many cakes they ate.

'I made them all,' she said. 'So it's nice to see them being eaten. I know you like them then.'

'We certainly do, Dimmy,' said Nora. The others giggled and looked at Miss Dimity. Was she going to be cross at being called Dimmy?

'Dear me,' she said, 'that's what I was called at school. It is nice to hear that old name again!'

So after that they all called her Dimmy, and the name suited her beautifully.

When they had eaten their tea Dimmy got up to clear away. She did all the cooking and housework herself.

'Would you like us to help you?' asked Peggy politely.

'Oh no, thank you,' said Dimmy, stacking up the cups and saucers. 'You've come here to have a holiday, not to help me. But there are one or two rules I want you to keep, all of you.'

'What are they?' asked Mike, rather alarmed. This sounded a bit like school to him.

'Oh, nothing very much,' said Dimmy, smiling. 'You must make your own beds each morning. You must be in good time for meals – though if you want to picnic out of doors you can tell me and I'll put you up lunch or tea any time you like. And the third thing is something your mother asked me – that is, you must be in bed by half-past eight.'

'All right, Dimmy,' said Mike. 'We'll keep the rules. We've all got watches, so we know the time. Now can we go and explore a bit?'

'Yes – go out for an hour, then come back in time for bed,' said Dimmy. 'I'll unpack for you, if you like.'

'Oh goody!' said Peggy, pleased. 'Thanks very much. Come on, you others!'

They all trooped out of the house and ran to the path that led down to the beach. It was a steep path, made of steps that were cut into the rock itself.

'It winds down like our tower staircase!' said Mike. 'Isn't it a steep cliff – and I say, just *look* at the colour of the sea! I've never seen such a blue.'

The sun was sinking in the west. To the east the sea was deep blue and calm. To the west it was full of a dancing golden light. The children laughed for joy and jumped down the last steps to the golden sand. It was studded with shells of all sorts.

'I'll be able to make a fine collection of shells,' said Mike, who loved to make collections of all kinds of things.

'I say! Look at those caves!' suddenly said Jack, and he pointed to the cliff behind them. The others looked. They saw big and small holes in the cliffs.

'Let's go and see them,' said Nora. She ran up to the cliff and peered inside one cave.

'Oooh!' she said. 'It's cold and dark in there.' She was right. It was. The sunshine could not get inside the deep caves, and they felt damp and mysterious.

'I wonder how far they go back,' said Mike. 'It would be fun to bring a torch and see.'

'We'll do that one day,' said Peggy. 'Now what about a paddle? Come on!'

They took off their sandals and splashed into the water. It was warm. They danced about in glee, and played 'catch' in the water. Nora fell over and soaked her dress.

Peggy squeezed it out, and then looked at her watch.

'Goodness, it's time we went back!' she said. 'We must hurry. Come on!'

They ran back to the cliff and climbed up the steep, narrow path in the rock, panting and puffing, for they were not yet used to it. Then down the garden they ran to the side-door of Peep-Hole. Miss Dimity was setting a simple supper for them of green lettuce and brown bread and butter, and barley water.

'Good old Dimmy!' cried Mike. 'Oh, this is a lovely place, Dimmy. There are dozens of caves down there on the beach.'

'I know,' said Dimmy. 'They are called the Spiggy Holes after a famous smuggler called Spiggy, who lived a hundred and fifty years ago. He used to live in that old house higher up the cliff. It is said that he used *this* house as a spy-place so that he might know when his smuggling boats were coming in.'

'Oooh! How exciting!' said Mike. 'Good old Spiggy!'

'He wasn't good,' said Miss Dimity sternly. 'He was very bad.'

'I wish there were smugglers nowadays,' said Peggy. 'Then perhaps we could spy on them and discover them. It would be most exciting.'

'Well, there are no smugglers in Spiggy Holes,' said Dimmy. 'Have you finished your supper? It is quite time you went up to bed. I suppose you can be trusted to wash and clean your teeth and all that without me seeing that you do?'

'Dimmy dear, *do* you suppose our teachers at school come and see that we do all that?' said Jack. 'It may surprise you to know that we are all of us over five years old.'

'It doesn't surprise me at all, you cheeky boy,' said Dimmy, poking him with a spoon, as he ran by her. 'Go along with you!'

They all went upstairs giggling. 'Dimmy is a good sort,' said Nora, as she undressed in her little round tower room with Peggy. 'She likes a bit of fun. Oh, I *do*

16

like this funny bedroom, with its four windows, don't you, Peggy?'

'Yes,' said Peggy. 'But the boys have got the best room – so high up like that. Let's go and say goodnight to them.'

They slipped on their dressing-gowns and climbed the winding stairs to the boys' room. Both the boys were in bed. 'We've come to say goodnight,' said Peggy. 'Isn't this a lovely place to stay in, Mike?'

'Lovely,' said Mike, with a huge yawn. 'I like a room where the sun shines in from dawn to dusk, and has four windows to peep through!'

Peggy went to the window that looked up the cliff, away from the sea.

'That old house looks spooky,' she said. 'I don't think I like it. Do you see its big tower, Mike? It is just like this little one, but taller and bigger. It seems as if that big tower is frowning down at ours.'

'You do have silly ideas, Peggy,' said Mike sleepily. 'We'll go and explore the grounds of the Old House sometime – and wouldn't it be fun if the house was empty and we could go inside and see what the tower there was like!'

'I wonder what Spiggy the Smuggler was like,' said Nora.

'You'll have Dimmy chasing after you with a hairbrush if you don't go to bed right now,' said Jack, burying his head in his pillow. 'I can't think why you are so wide awake. Do go to bed.'

'All right,' said Peggy. 'Goodnight. See you tomorrow, sleepy heads!'

She and Nora slipped down the winding stairs into their own room. They got into bed. They were tiny little beds, but very comfortable.

'Now I'm going to think about all we've done today,' began Nora. But before she had thought more than twelve words her mind floated off into sleep, and she didn't move until the morning. The sun came in from the opposite window then, and Peggy and Nora were awakened by somebody tickling them.

'Oooh, don't!' squealed Nora. 'Mike, stop! What do you want?'

'Come and bathe before breakfast,' said Mike. 'Get up, lazybones. It's seven o'clock. Breakfast isn't till eight, so we've lots of time.'

Nora and Peggy sat up, quite wide awake. They looked round their sunny room with its four quaint windows. They could see four bits of bright blue sky, and they could hear the sound of the waves breaking at the cliff-foot. They felt so full of happiness that they had to sing.

> *'Here we are at Spiggy Holes,*
> *Here we are at Spiggy –*
> *Here we are at Spiggy Holes,*
> *Pop goes the weasel!'*

yelled Nora to the tune of 'Pop goes the Weasel'.

The others took up the silly song and they all went downstairs in their swimsuits, roaring the tune. Miss Dimity put her head out of the kitchen.

'Dear me, it's you!' she said. 'I thought it was the

canary singing.' —

The children squealed with laughter and rushed down the steep path to the beach. They flung themselves into the water.

'Now our holidays really *have* begun!' said Mike, as he splashed Peggy. 'What fun we're going to have!'

# Inside the Old House

The first few days of the summer holiday slipped away happily. The children explored the beach, which was a most exciting one, but rather dangerous. The tide came right up to the cliffs when it was in, and filled most of the caves.

'We shall have to be careful not to get caught in any of these caves when the tide is coming in,' said Jack. 'It would be very difficult to get out.'

Miss Dimity warned them too, and told them many stories of people who had explored the caves, forgetting about the tide, and who had had to be rescued by boats when they found that they could not get out of the caves.

The bathing was lovely at low tide. The children had to promise not to bathe at high tide, for then the waves were very big, and Dimmy was afraid the children might be dashed against the rocks. But it was lovely to bathe at low tide. The rock pools were deep and warm. The sand was smooth and golden, and felt pleasant to their bare feet.

'You need not wear your shoes here,' Dimmy told them. 'No trippers ever come to Spiggy Holes, leaving their litter and broken glass behind them!'

So they went barefoot, and loved to feel the sand

between their toes. The farm lad, who came to do Dimmy's garden for her, lent them his boat, and the four children had a wonderful time at low tide, boating around the rocks and all about the craggy coast.

One day there was a very high tide indeed. The waves splashed against the cliffs and all the caves were full of water. There was nothing to do down on the beach, because, for one thing, there *was* no beach, and for another Dimmy said it was dangerous to go down the cliff path when the tides were high because the spray made the path slippery, and they might easily slip down and fall into the high water.

'Well, what shall we do then?' said Jack, wandering out into the garden, and picking some pea-pods. He split the pods and emptied the peas into his mouth. Dimmy had a lovely garden – full of peas and beans and lettuces and gooseberries and late cherries and early plums. None of the children could help picking something as they went through it every day.

'I know what we'll do!' said Mike. 'We'll go and explore the garden of the Old House. Come on!'

They passed the farm lad, George, who was busy digging up some potatoes. Nora called to him.

'Hello! We're going to explore the garden of the Old House. Nobody lives there, do they, George?'

'That house has been empty this twenty years,' said George. 'Maybe more. The garden is like a forest!'

'It will be fun to explore it then,' said Peggy. They ran up the slope of the cliff towards the Old House. They were all in sunsuits and shady hats, but even so they were very hot. Soon they came to a high wall that

21

ran all round the big garden of the Old House.

'We can't climb over this,' said Jack, looking up at the wall, which was three times as tall as he was. 'What are we going to do?'

'What about going in through the gates?' said Mike, with a grin. 'Or do you feel it would be more exciting to break your leg trying to climb that wall, Jack?'

Everybody laughed. 'Well, it *would* be more exciting to climb the wall,' said Jack, giving Mike a friendly punch. 'But we'll go and find the gates.'

The gates were locked, but the children easily climbed over them. They jumped to the ground on the other side.

There was a long, dark drive in front of them, winding its way below tall, overhanging trees to the front door. The drive was completely overgrown with nettles and thistles, and the children stopped in dismay.

'I say!' said Jack. 'We want to be dressed in macintoshes and boots to make our way through these stinging, prickly things! If we push through them we shall get terribly stung!'

'Well, look,' said Nora, pointing to the left. 'There's a better way off to the left there – just tall grass, and no nettles. Let's go that way.'

So they went to the left, making their way through shrubberies and overgrown beds. It was a very large garden, and very exciting, for there were all kinds of fruit trees that had not been pruned for years, but whose fruit was sweet and delicious.

The children picked some ripe plums and enjoyed the sweet juice. 'Nobody lives here, so it can't matter having a few plums,' said Nora. 'The wasps would have them if we didn't. Isn't it hot in this garden!'

'Let's go and see what the house is like,' said Jack. So they pushed their way through the long sprays of overgrown rosebushes and went up to the house. It was built of white stone, and was very solid and strong. It had rather small windows, very dirty indeed, and the rooms looked dark and dreary when the children looked through the glass.

They came to the round tower built on to one side of the house, just as the tower of Peep-Hole was built on to Miss Dimity's house.

'This is an enormous tower,' said Mike, in surprise. 'It's three times as big as ours! My word, I'd like to go up it! The view over the sea must be marvellous!'

'Let's see if we can get into the house,' said Peggy. She tried some of the windows, but they were fast shut. Mike tried a door set deep into the wall of the tower but that was locked and bolted inside.

Then Jack gave a shout. He had found an old broken ladder lying on the ground and had set it up beside the wall of the round tower. It just reached to a small window.

'I believe that window could be opened,' said Jack. 'Come and hold the ladder, Mike. The rungs don't look too good to me.'

Mike held the ladder and Jack went carefully up it.

One of the rungs broke as he trod on it and he nearly fell. The ladder wobbled dangerously, but Mike was holding it tightly, so Jack was quite all right.

He climbed up to the windowsill and tried to pull the

window open. 'The catch is broken!' he said. 'I believe I can get the window open if I try long enough. It's stuck hard.'

'I'll hold the ladder tight,' Mike shouted back. 'Shake the window and bang the bottom part, Jack. Nora, help me to hold the ladder. Jack's shaking the window so hard that the ladder is swinging about! I don't want him

24

sitting on my head suddenly!'

There was a shout from above and the ladder wobbled again. 'I've got it open!' cried Jack. 'It came up with a rush!'

'We'll climb up the ladder then,' said Nora, in excitement.

'No,' said Jack, leaning out of the window. He had climbed in through it. 'That ladder's too dangerous for you all to use. I'll pop down and unlock the door in the tower, just near you.'

'Right,' said Mike, and he took the ladder away and threw it down on the ground again. Jack disappeared. They could hear him running down the stairs of the tower. Then they heard him undoing bolts, and turning a rusty key. He pulled at the door and Mike pushed. It opened so suddenly that Jack sat down in the dust, and Mike flew in through the door as if he were running a race!

The girls followed, laughing at the two boys. Jack got up and dusted himself. 'Let's go up the tower first,' he said. 'Look at the walls! They seem about four feet thick! Gosh, they knew how to build in the old days!'

The tower was very solid indeed. It had a small winding staircase that ran round and round as it went upwards. There were four rooms in the tower, one on top of the other.

'They are all quite round,' said Jack. 'Just as ours are in the Peep-Hole tower. I say! What a magnificent view you get over the sea from this top room!'

The children stood in silence and looked out of the window over the sea. It shimmered there for miles in the sun, purple blue, with tiny white flecks where the water washed over hidden rocks.

'You can see the tower of Peep-Hole very well from here,' said Mike. 'The two towers must have been built in these special positions so that the smugglers could signal to each other. If one of us were in our tower today we could easily wave a hanky to the others here, and it would be seen perfectly.'

'Mike! Jack! I can hear something!' said Nora suddenly. She had very sharp ears.

The others looked startled. 'Whatever do you mean, Nora?' said Jack. 'I can hear things too – the birds singing, and the faraway sound of the sea!'

'I don't mean those,' said Nora. 'I am sure I heard voices.'

'Voices! In an old empty house that hasn't been lived in for years!' said Jack, laughing.

'I tell you I *did*,' said Nora. She suddenly pointed out through one of the tower windows.' Just look down there!' she said. 'You can see the front gate from here – look at it!'

The others looked, and their eyes opened wide in surprise.

'The front gate is open!' said Mike. 'And it was fast locked when we climbed over it! Nora is right. She must have heard somebody.'

'Perhaps it is somebody come to look over the house to buy it,' said Nora. 'Oh dear – we oughtn't to be here, I'm sure. And I wish we hadn't eaten those plums now. Let's go quickly.'

The others could hear the voices very clearly now

too. Jack looked alarmed. 'I believe they're in the tower already,' he said. 'They must have come into the house by the front door and gone round to the tower.'

'They are coming up the stairway!' whispered Peggy, her hand half over her mouth. 'Sh! Don't talk any more. Maybe they won't come right up to the top.'

The voices came clearly up the stairway. One was a man's and one was a woman's.

'This tower is the very place,' said the man's deep voice, which did not sound quite English.

'Nobody would ever guess,' said the woman's voice, and she laughed. It was not a kind laugh. The strangers went into the room below the top one and the woman exclaimed at the view.

'Isn't it marvellous! And so lonely too. Not a house within miles except that little one down there – it's called the Peep-Hole, isn't it? And the old farmhouse four miles off. It's just right for us, Felipe.'

'Yes,' said the man. 'Come along – we've seen all we need.'

The children breathed a sigh of relief. So the people weren't coming up to their room after all.

'Well, I'd very much like to see the view from the topmost room of all,' said the woman. 'Also, that's the room we'd use, isn't it?'

'Very well. Come along, then,' said the man. 'But hurry, please, because we haven't long.'

The footsteps came up and up. The children didn't know what to do, so they simply stood together and waited for the small but strong door to be opened. It swung inwards, and they saw a golden-haired woman looking at them, and a man with a very dark skin behind her.

'Well!' said the woman in astonishment and anger. 'What are *you* doing here?'

'We just came to have a look at the garden and the tower of the Old House,' said Jack. 'We are staying at the Peep-Hole.'

The man came into the room and scowled at them. 'You've no right to get into empty houses. We are going to buy this house – and if we catch any of you in the house or garden again we'll give you a good hiding. Do you understand – because we mean it! Now clear out!'

The children were frightened. They tore down the winding staircase and out into the sunlight without a word. They had seldom been spoken to like that before.

'Let's go and tell Dimmy,' said Nora. 'Do hurry!'

# Can They Be Smugglers?

The four children rushed out of the front gate and didn't stop till they got to the Peep-Hole. How nice and friendly it seemed, and how kind Dimmy looked as she stood picking peas for supper in the garden!

'Dimmy!' cried Nora, rushing up to her. 'Some people are going to buy the Old House.'

Dimmy looked astonished. 'Whatever for?' she asked. 'It's no use except for a school or for a hotel or something like that – it's so lonely for an ordinary family.'

'Dimmy, they are odd people,' said Jack, and he told what had happened. 'Do you suppose they really *would* punish us if we go there again?'

'Quite likely,' said Dimmy, going indoors with the peas. 'If they are buying the house it will be theirs. So keep away from it. Surely you've got plenty to do without going wandering over *that* old place!'

'Well, you see, it's a mysterious sort of place, somehow,' said Jack. 'It looks as if anything might happen there. I keep looking at it and wondering about it.'

'So do I,' said Nora. 'I don't like the Old House – but I can't help thinking about it.'

'Rubbish!' said Miss Dimity. 'No doubt these people will move in and make it a holiday place, and it will be just as ordinary as Peep-Hole.'

'Let's go and bathe,' said Mike suddenly. 'Don't let's think about it any more. They are horrid people, and we'll forget them.'

They fetched their towels in silence. They had all had a shock, for never had they thought that anyone could speak to them so fiercely, or threaten them so unkindly. However, when they were splashing in the warm water they forgot the strange old house and the strange couple that were going to buy it, and shouted happily to one another.

But they had another shock when they went in to their tea that afternoon. They saw a car outside the door, and inside it was sitting the same yellow-haired woman they had seen in the Old House! She looked at them without smiling.

The children went indoors, puzzled – and they walked straight into the dark-skinned man! He was standing just inside the sitting-room door, listening to Dimmy.

'Oh! Sorry!' said Jack. 'I didn't know you had a visitor, Dimmy.'

'He's just going,' said Dimmy, who looked quite worried. 'Go and tidy yourselves for tea.'

As the children turned to go they heard the man speak again.

'But why will you not sell me this little house? I am offering far more money to you for it than you will ever get when you want to sell it!'

'It has been in my family for two hundred years,' said Dimmy firmly. 'It is true that I only live here in the summertime, but I love it and I will not part from it.'

'Well, will you rent it to me for twelve months?' asked the man.

'No,' said Miss Dimity. 'I have never let it, and I don't want to.'

'Very well,' said the man angrily. 'Do as you please. But I think you are very foolish.'

'I'm afraid I don't really mind what you think about me,' said Dimmy with a laugh. 'Now, please go. The children want their tea.'

'Oh, the children – yes, that reminds me,' said the man sternly. 'Keep them out of the Old House from now on, or they will get into serious trouble. I'm not going to have badly behaved children running all over my house and grounds.'

'They are not badly behaved,' said Dimmy, 'and they didn't know you were going to buy it till today. Good-day.'

She showed the man out of the door. He went to the car frowning, started it with a great noise and roared off down the country lane.

'Sort of fellow who likes a car to sound like a hundred aeroplanes,' said Mike in disgust, looking out of his tower window. 'You know, Jack, there's something funny about that man. Why does he want to buy the Old House – *and* the Peep-Hole, too? Do you suppose he's going to do something that he wants no one to know of? This would be a marvellous place to do a bit of smuggling, for instance.'

'People use aeroplanes for that sort of thing nowadays,' said Jack. 'No – 1 just can't imagine what he's going to do here – but I'd dearly like to find out. And if

Mr Felipe, or whatever his name is, is up to something funny, I vote we find out what it is!'

'Yes, let's,' said Nora excitedly. She and Peggy had come up to the boys' room to brush their hair. 'I feel as if something is going to happen. Don't you?'

'I do rather,' said Jack. 'Though it may all turn out to be quite ordinary.'

'Children! Are you never coming down to tea?' called Miss Dimity. 'I suppose you don't want any jam scones today?'

'Yes we do, yes we do!' yelled the children, rushing down the winding stairs. 'Is there cream with them?'

There was. Dimmy poured out their milk and handed round the new scones thickly spread with raspberry jam.

'Dimmy, who was that man?' asked Jack.

'He said his name was Mr Felipe Diaz,' said Dimmy, eating a scone. 'Fancy him thinking I'd let him have the Peep-Hole! I certainly wouldn't sell my old home to a person like Mr Diaz!'

'We think he's up to no good,' said Jack, taking a second scone. 'And if he is, Dimmy, *we* are going to find out what's wrong!'

'Now don't you do anything of the sort,' said Dimmy at once. 'He's a man of his word, and if he says he'll punish you if you trespass on his grounds you may be sure you'll get into trouble if you disobey. Keep away from the Old House. Don't even peep over the wall.'

The children said nothing. They didn't want to make any promises, because they never broke a promise, and it would spoil things if they had to promise Dimmy never to go near the Old House.

They ate a huge tea, and not a single scone or cake was left. 'You made too few scones, Dimmy dear,' said Jack, getting up.

'Oh no, I didn't,' said Dimmy. 'You ate too many! I am just wondering whether I shall bother to think about supper for you – I am sure you couldn't possibly eat any more today.'

The children laughed. They knew Dimmy was only teasing them. 'We're going out in George's boat,' said Jack. 'Why don't you come with us, Dimmy? We'd love to have you.'

Dimmy shook her head. 'I've plenty to do,' she said. 'Go off and enjoy yourselves and see if you can possibly get an appetite for supper!'

The children shot off to get George's boat. He kept it tied to a rough little wooden pier in a cove nearby. He used it for fishing and it was a good, strong little boat.

'George, did you see anything of the people who are going to buy the Old House?' asked Jack eagerly.

'Yes,' said George, who was mending his fishing lines. 'They came and asked me to tidy up the garden a bit and to get a couple of women from the nearest village to scrub down the house. And they wanted to know a tidy lot about the coast around here!'

'Did they? What for?' asked Mike.

'That's what *I'd* like to know!' said George, with a laugh. 'That man's up to no good, I reckon! He wanted me to sell him my boat too, when I told him it was the only one hereabouts.'

'Oh, George! You didn't sell it to him, did you?' cried Jack in dismay.

'Of course not,' said George. 'I wouldn't part with my boat, not for a hundred pounds! I don't think they wanted the boat to use themselves though – I just think they didn't want me rowing round about this coast for a bit.'

'George! Do you think they are smugglers then?' cried Mike. 'I thought smugglers used aeroplanes, not boats nowadays.'

'They've got some little game on,' said George, packing up his nets neatly into the bottom of the boat. 'But I'm not going to help them by selling my boat, I'm going to keep my eyes open.'

'So are we, George, so are we!' cried the four children excitedly. They told him all about their adventure in the Old House that day. George listened. He got into his boat, which was floating by the side of the little jetty, and beckoned to the children to get in.

'You come along with me and I'll show you something,' he said. They all tumbled in, and Jack and Mike took an oar each. George had two. They rowed out on the calm sea, bumping a little on the waves that ran round the rocks here and there.

'We've got to row a good way,' said George. 'I reckon we can just do it before supper. Right round the cliff there, look – and beyond it – and then round the next crag too. It's a goodish way.'

It was lovely on the sea in the evening. The children took turns at rowing. The sun sank lower. The boat rounded the big cliff, went across the next bay, and rounded a great craggy head of rock that stood well out into the sea. Beyond that the cliff fell almost down to

sea-level before it rose again.

George took the boat well out to sea then – and suddenly he pulled in his oars, shaded his eyes with his hand, and looked over the land to the north-west.

'Now you look over there,' he said, 'and tell me what you can see.'

The children looked. Jack gave a shout. 'Why, we can see the topmost window of the Old House from here – and we can see the topmost window of our own tower too! The cliffs seem to fall away in a more or less straight line from here, and the towers can just be seen.'

'Yes,' said George. 'And in smuggling days a ship could come and anchor out here, right out of sight of Spiggy Holes, and could come in at night when a light shone in those towers! Old man Spiggy used to light the lamp when it was safe, and it used to wink out at the smuggling ships here, and in they'd ride on the tide, unseen by anyone!'

'It does sound exciting,' said Jack. 'Do you suppose Mr Felipe Diaz is going to use the tower for the same thing, George?'

'Oh no!' said George. 'But we'll keep our eyes open, shall we?'

'Yes, rather!' cried all the children, and rowed back to supper as fast as they could.

# The Light in the Tower

The next few days the children kept a sharp eye on the Old House. They saw smoke rising from two of the chimneys and guessed that women were at work cleaning the big place. George also went up and tried to clear the weeds from the drive, and he told the children that the new people were coming in the very next week.

'They seem in a mighty hurry to come in,' he said. 'Why, that place wants painting from top to bottom – and they're not going to have anything done except that the big boiler is to be put right!'

The children bathed and paddled, fished and boated as much as ever, but the day that the new people moved into the Old House all four of them went to hide themselves in an enormous oak tree that grew not far from the gates.

They climbed up into the tree, settled themselves down on two broad branches, leaned comfortably against the trunk of the tree, and sat there, whispering and waiting.

Presently a large removal van came along the road, and then another – but that was all.

'Funny!' said Jack, in surprise. 'Only two vans of furniture for that enormous house! They must just be furnishing a small part of it.'

The vans moved in through the gates, stopped in front of the house, and the men began to unload. Then the big car belonging to Mr Felipe Diaz came tearing along, and, just under the tree where the children hid, it had to stop, to allow a tradesman's van to pass out of the gates.

In the car was Mr Diaz, the yellow-haired woman, a chauffeur as dark as Mr Diaz, and a sleepy-eyed young man who lolled back in the car, talking to the woman.

'Well,' said Mr Diaz, hopping out of the car, and beckoning to the young man to come with him. 'Here we are! You go on to the house, Anna. Luiz and I are just going to walk round the walls of the place to see that they are all right.'

The car moved in through the gates. The two men stood underneath the tree, talking in low tones. The children could hear every word.

'This is as safe a place as anywhere in the country,' said Mr Diaz. 'See that tower? Well, the boat can hang about right out of sight till we light a signal in the tower. Then it can come slipping in, and nobody will ever know. We shall be copying the old smugglers, Luiz – but our goods are not quite the same! Ha, ha!'

Luiz laughed too. 'Come on,' he said. 'I want to see the place. When are the dogs coming?'

Mr Diaz murmured something that the children couldn't hear, and the two went off round the walls of the Old House's garden. The children, who had hardly dared to breathe whilst the men had stood beneath the tree, looked at one another in the greatest excitement.

'Did you hear?' whispered Mike. 'They're going to use a boat – and put a signal into the tower! It's just like the old days!'

'But are they smugglers then?' asked Nora, puzzled. 'And what are the "goods" they spoke of?'

'*I* don't know,' said Mike. 'But I'm jolly well going to find out. This is about the most exciting thing that has happened to us since we ran away long ago to our secret island!'

'I love adventures,' said Jack. 'But look here – we've got to be jolly careful of these people. If they think we even guess that they're up to something, there'll be a whole heap of trouble for us!'

'We'll be careful,' said Nora, and she began to climb down the tree. 'Come on! I'm tired of being up here.'

'Nora! Don't be an idiot!' whispered Jack, as loudly as he dared. 'Come back – we haven't looked to see if it's safe to get down!'

But Nora slipped at that moment, slid down the last bit of tree trunk, and landed on her hands and knees on the ground below the tree. And at that very moment Mr Diaz and Luiz came back from their walk round the high walls of the grounds!

They saw Nora, and Mr Diaz frowned. 'Come here!' he shouted. Nora was too afraid to go to him, and too afraid to run away! She just stood there and stared. The others up the tree stayed as still as mice, wondering what Nora was going to do.

Mr Diaz came up to poor Nora and shouted at her. 'What are you doing here? Didn't I say that you children were not to come round the Old House?' He took hold of Nora's shoulder and shook her.

'Where are the others? Are they anywhere about?'

Nora knew that Mr Diaz hadn't seen her fall from the tree, and she was glad. If only he didn't look up and see the others!

'Please let me go,' she said, half crying. 'I just came for a walk up here. I haven't been inside the gates.'

'You just try coming inside the grounds!' said Mr Diaz fiercely. He gave her another shake. 'Now, go home. And tell the others that if *they* come for walks up here they will soon feel very sorry for themselves. I keep a cane for tiresome children!'

'I'll go and tell the others,' said Nora, and she sped away down the slope of the cliff as if she were going to find Peggy, Jack, and Mike straightaway.

'That's given her a good fright,' said Luiz, with a

40

sleepy grin. 'We don't want any sharp-eyed kids about, Felipe! Well, when the two dogs come they'll keep everyone away. They'll bite anyone on sight!'

The two men went through the gate laughing together. When they were safely out of sight, Jack spoke.

'A nice pleasant pair, aren't they?' he whispered to the others. 'Nora was pretty sharp the way she shot off like that – it looked exactly as if she was going to find us – and yet there we were above dear Mr Diaz's head all the time! He'd only got to look up and see my big feet!'

I want to get down as soon as I can,' said Peggy, who felt that if anyone *did* happen to see them up the tree they would be well trapped. 'Is it safe to slip down now, Jack?'

Jack parted the leaves and peered all round. 'Yes,' he said. 'Come on, down we go!'

One by one they slipped down, and then shot off down the slope, keeping behind the big gorse bushes as much as they could in case any of the people of the Old House caught sight of them. They guessed that Nora would be waiting for them at the Peep-Hole.

She was – but she was crying bitterly.

'Don't cry, Nora,' said Jack, putting his arm round her. 'Were you very frightened?'

'I'm n-n-n-ot crying b-b-b-because I was frightened,' sobbed Nora, 'I'm c-c-c-rying because I was such an idiot – slipping down out of the tree like that, and nearly spoiling everything.'

'Well, that was really very silly of you,' said Mike. 'But you didn't give us away, thank goodness – you were quite sharp, Nora. So cheer up – but you'd better be careful next time.'

'Jack shall be captain,' said Peggy. 'He always was on the secret island – and he shall be now. He shall take charge of this adventure, and we'll do what he says.'

'All right,' said Nora, cheering up and putting away her hanky. 'I'll always do what the captain says.'

'Do you think we ought to tell Dimmy about this adventure?' said Mike.

'No, I don't,' said Jack at once. 'She is awfully nice – but she might be frightened. She might even forbid us to try and find out anything. We'll keep this secret all to ourselves – though perhaps we might get George to help us later on.'

'Did you hear what they said about the boat coming in?' said Mike. 'We'll watch for that, anyway! We can take it in turns to sit up each night in the top bedroom of our own tower and watch for a light in the tower of the big house. When we see it, we'll slip down to the beach, hide in a cave, and watch the boat coming in – and maybe we'll see what the mysterious "goods" are that Mr Diaz is smuggling in!'

'It's getting very exciting,' said Peggy, not quite sure whether she liked it or not. 'We shall have to be awfully careful that we're not seen or caught.'

George told the children that the furniture had been put into only eight of the twenty rooms of the Old House.

'The tower rooms have been furnished,' he said. 'I found that out from one of the women who is cleaning the place. So they are going to use the tower.'

'Yes – they are going to use the tower!' said Mike, looking at the others. But they did not tell George what they knew. He was very nice – but he was almost grown-up and he might think, perhaps, they should tell Miss Dimity – and they did so want to follow the adventure themselves and find out everything before any grown-ups came into it.

That night the children undressed in great excitement. Jack was to take the first watch, from ten o'clock to twelve o'clock. Then Mike was to watch from twelve to two and Nora from two to four. By that time it would be daylight and there would be no need to watch.

The next night Peggy was to begin the watch. 'We must sit by this window, and keep our eyes on the tower of the Old House,' said Jack. 'If any of us sees a light flashing or burning there, he must wake the others at once – and then we'll all creep down to the beach, hide in a cave and see if we can spot the boat coming in.'

Peggy and Nora went down to their bedroom. They found it difficult to go to sleep. Mike got into bed and talked to Jack, but they both fell asleep very soon. Jack had set the alarm clock to wake him at ten.

'R-r-r-r-r-ring!' It went off shrilly at ten o'clock. Jack sat up and switched it off. 'Good thing Dimmy gave us our rooms right away in this tower,' he thought to himself. 'She would be woken too, if we slept anywhere near her. Mike, are you awake? Well, go to sleep again. I'm going to watch now, and I'll wake you at twelve.'

Jack put on a dressing gown, and sat down by the window that looked towards the tower of the Old House. It was a dark, cloudy night. Jack could not make out the

43

tower, stare as he might.

'Well, I should see it if it had a light in it,' he thought.

An owl hooted in a distant wood. A moth fluttered in a corner near Jack's head and made him jump. He yawned. After the first five minutes, it was rather boring to sit and look at dark nothingness.

He was glad when it was time to wake Mike. Mike stumbled sleepily out of bed, dragged on his dressing gown, and went to sit by the window. Jack tumbled into bed thankfully and was asleep in a second.

Mike sat and stared sleepily at the tower of the Old House. He could just see it now, for the sky had cleared. The tower was dark. Mike felt his eyes closing and he jerked his head up. He got up to walk about, afraid that he might fall asleep in the chair.

When his two hours were almost up, he heard a sound in the bedroom, and a hand touched his shoulder. Mike almost jumped out of his skin. He hit out and struck something soft.

'Oh!' said Nora's voice. 'You hurt me, Mike! I've just come up to tell you it's my turn to watch.'

'Well, what do you want to come creeping in like that for, and make me jump!' said Mike crossly. 'I thought you were a smuggler or something!'

Nora giggled and took her seat by the window. 'Get into bed,' she said. 'It's my turn now. Oooh, I do feel important!'

That night nothing happened – neither did anything happen the next night or the next – but on the fourth night there was great excitement. A light flashed in the tower at midnight! There it was, as plain as could be!

# A Strange Discovery

It was Peggy who first saw the light flashing in the tower of the Old House. Mike had had the first watch that night, and Peggy had come up from her room about one minute before midnight to take her turn at watching.

She whispered a few words to Mike, and took her seat by the window.

'There hasn't been a sign of anything,' Mike said in a low voice, and he threw off his dressing gown to get into bed. 'This is the fourth night we've watched – it's a bit boring, I think. Do you suppose that...'

But just at that moment Peggy gave such a loud squeal that Mike jumped. 'Mike! Oooh, look! Mike! There's a light in the tower. It's just come, this very moment!'

Mike ran to the window, almost falling over a chair on the way. Jack awoke at the noise.

'Yes!' said Mike. 'It's a light! Jack! Jack! Come and look!'

Jack jumped out of bed and ran to the window. Sure enough, there was a light in the distant tower – a light that dipped and flashed and dipped and flashed.

'They are signalling,' said Jack, in excitement. 'The boat must be standing out to sea watching for the signal, right beyond that rocky crag we sailed round.'

'Shall we get on our things and slip down to the

beach?' said Mike, so excited that he could hardly stand still.

'Yes,' said Jack. 'Peggy, wake Nora. There's no hurry, because if that light has only just shone out of the tower, it will take some time for the boat to get round to Spiggy Holes. We've plenty of time to dress properly.'

Peggy flew down the winding staircase to tell Nora, who was still sleeping soundly. Peggy shook her, and Nora woke up in a hurry.

'Nora! The light's in the tower! Hurry and get dressed, because we're all going to creep down to the beach and hide in a cave to watch,' said Peggy. Nora almost fell out of bed in her excitement. They put on their clothes in the dark, for Jack had forbidden lights of any sort in their tower, in case they should be seen from the Old House.

'If we can see their light, they could see ours,' said Jack.

'True, Captain!' said Mike and dressed himself at top speed. He put on both his socks inside out, and buttoned his coat up wrong – but who minded?

They were all ready in five minutes. Jack took his torch and gave one to Peggy for the girls. They all crept down the staircase, out of the little tower door, and down the garden path, where the smell of honeysuckle came to them.

'Nora's got on her bedroom slippers,' said Peggy, with a giggle. 'She couldn't find her others.'

'Sh!' said Jack sharply. 'Other people may be about, remember. We mustn't be seen or heard.'

They went as quietly as they could down the rocky

path to the beach. The tide was half in and half out. The moon swam out from behind a cloud and lighted up the shore for the children. Jack stopped and looked out over the sea.

'No sign of any boat yet,' he whispered. 'Let's get into one of the nearest caves and get settled before anyone arrives. I expect the people from the Old House will come down to the beach soon.'

The children went into a small cave not far from the steep cliff path. They thought that if they hid there they could easily see who came or went up the cliff. They sat on the dry sand on the floor of the cave and waited, speaking in whispers. Nora was shaking with excitement. She said her knees wouldn't keep still.

Suddenly the children heard voices, and they stiffened in surprise. The voices were to the right of them. Jack cautiously peeped out of the cave when the moon went behind a cloud.

'I believe it's the man called Felipe Diaz and that sleepy-looking chap called Luiz,' whispered Jack.

'But, Jack, how in the world did they get on to the beach?' whispered back Mike. 'We didn't see them come down the cliff path – and that's the only way down on to the beach for a couple of miles! The cliffs are much too steep anywhere else to get down to the shore.'

'That's funny,' said Jack. 'They couldn't have been here already, surely, or we'd have seen them. Perhaps they were waiting in a cave. Good gracious, I hope they didn't spot us!'

Nora went hot and cold when she heard Jack say that. Mike shook his head.

'If they'd seen us they'd have rushed us off the beach at once,' he said. 'They wouldn't want us to see what was happening tonight. Listen! What's that!'

The children listened – and over the black and silver water they heard the sound of a low humming.

'It's a motor-boat!' said Jack, in an excited whisper. 'It's been waiting out yonder, round the crag, for the signal. Now it's coming in! Watch out, everyone. See all you can.'

The children stood up and craned their necks round the rocky edges of the cave. The moon came out for a moment, and coming nearer and nearer to the shore a large motor-boat could be seen, glinting in the mooning. Its hum was loud in the stillness of the night.

It shut off its engine and ran gently into the little cove where George kept his boat. The children could no longer see it.

'It must be by George's small wooden jetty,' whispered Jack. 'Well, we shall see what kind of goods the smugglers are bringing in, when they pass us on their way to the cliff path.'

They all waited impatiently. The sound of hushed voices came to them, and the thud of the boat against

the wooden pier. The children waited and waited. Then there came the sound of humming once again, and the motor-boat slid out of the cove and made its way swiftly out to sea and round the rocky headlands.

'They'll be coming by in a second,' said Jack. 'Now be quiet as mice, everyone – don't sneeze or cough for goodness sake!'

Nora at once felt as if she was going to sneeze. She took out her hanky and buried her face in it. How dreadful if she gave their hiding place away just at this most important moment!

But the sneeze didn't come – and nobody came. Not a shadow passed in front of the children's cave. Not even a voice could be heard now.

After half an hour, the children became impatient.

'Jack, what's happened, do you suppose?' whispered Nora.

'Can't imagine,' said Jack. Then a thought struck him. 'I say! I wonder if the boat came to fetch anyone! We shouldn't see them come by if they'd gone in the boat!'

'Well, then, we might as well go out and look round a bit,' said Mike. 'Can we, Jack?'

'All right,' said Jack. 'But for goodness sake be quiet!'

They made their way softly to the little cove where the wooden pier stood. George's boat was beside it. Jack shone his torch on the ground and pointed out the footsteps in the sand.

'Let's follow them backwards and see where they come from,' said Mike. 'I simply can't understand how those men came down to the beach tonight without us seeing them pass.'

So, with the help of the torches the children followed two pairs of footsteps from the cove, round the beach – and into a big cave!

'So they must have been hiding here all the time!' said Jack.

'Look,' said Mike, in a puzzled voice, swinging his torch all over the sandy beach. 'There are no more footsteps beyond this cave – they didn't come to the cave by the cliff path, that's certain. Then how did they come?'

'Jack! Mike! There must be a secret passage from the Old House to the beach!' suddenly said Nora, in such a loud whisper that the others jumped.

'Sh!' said Jack. Then he too began to whisper loudly. 'I believe Nora's right! Of course! There's a secret passage from the shore to the Old House! Why didn't I think of it before! My goodness, Nora, that was smart of you to think of that.'

'The passage must begin in this cave, where the men's footsteps go,' said Nora, pleased and excited to think that Jack thought she was smart. 'Let's go in and explore.'

'And walk straight into Mr Diaz and his friend Luiz!' said Jack. 'No, thank you. Besides, I'd prefer to do it in daytime. It's a bit too creepy now. Come on, let's go back to bed and talk.'

They all went back up the steep cliff path, through the scented garden and into their tower. The girls curled up in one bed in the top room and the boys in the other.

And they talked. *How* they talked! They were so thrilled with the night's adventure that it was dawn before they thought of really going to bed.

'You see, what happened was they signalled to the boat to come in with the smuggled goods, whatever they were,' said Jack, for the twentieth time, 'and Mr Diaz and his friend slipped down from the Old House to the shore by the secret passage that leads to that cave – and then they took the goods up that way back to the Old House. So we never saw them.'

'*When* can we explore the cave for that secret passage, Jack?' said Peggy longingly.

'Tomorrow!' said Jack, hugging his knees, as he sat in Mike's bed.

'Today you mean!' said Mike, with a laugh, and he pointed to where the eastern sky was beginning to shine with a silvery light. 'It's today *now*. Come on, we really *must* go to sleep for a bit!'

The girls went down to their room. The boys settled into their beds and were asleep in a few seconds. It seemed as if they had only been in bed for a few minutes when Dimmy awakened them at half-past seven.

'Are you *never* going to wake today?' she said in amazement. 'Did you keep awake half the night, you naughty children?'

'Perhaps we did, Dimmy, perhaps we did!' said Jack, with a laugh – and not another word would he say to explain why they were all such sleepyheads that morning!

# The Secret Passage!

The children were half sleepy, half excited at breakfast-time. Dimmy couldn't make them out at all.

'I don't understand what's the matter with you all today,' she said, as she passed them their cocoa. 'First you yawn, then you giggle, then you rub your hands together in glee, then you yawn again. Are you planning any mischief?'

'Oh no, Dimmy,' said everyone together.

'Well, see you don't,' said Dimmy.

'Dimmy, would you give us a picnic lunch, please?' said Jack. 'We'd like to be out till tea.'

'Very well,' said Dimmy. 'You shall have some little veal and ham pies that I made yesterday, some ginger cake, and some ripe plums and lemonade. Will that do? Oh, and you can have some hard-boiled eggs, too, if you like.'

'Lovely!' said everybody. Nora got up and hugged Dimmy. 'You're a dear!' she said. 'It's lovely staying with you!'

Dimmy prepared their lunch whilst the children collected electric torches, and also candles and matches in case their torches failed. They talked excitedly. It was lovely to be going to find a secret passage.

Dimmy gave them the lunch done up in two kit-bags.

Jack put one on his back and Mike put the other on his. They called goodbye and ran off down the garden path to the cliff. Down the steep rocky steps they went, on to the beach.

The sea had been right up to the cliff and had washed away the footsteps of the night before. But the children knew which cave the men had come from and they made their way there, first looking to see that nobody else was on the beach too.

They came to the cave. The entrance was large and open. The cave ran back a good way, and was very dark and damp. Seaweed grew from the walls, and at the foot the red and green sea anemones grew, like lumps of jelly, waiting for the tide to sweep into the cave again so that they might open like flowers.

The children switched on their torches. They swung them here and there, all around the cave, looking for the passage that led from the cave.

At first they could find nothing at all. 'It's nothing but walls, walls, walls,' said Mike, flashing his torch round the damp rock that made the sides of the cave. 'And at the back it just ends in rock too. Oh dear – I wonder if after all there *isn't* a passage!'

'Look here!' shouted Jack suddenly. 'What's this?' He held his torch fairly high up one wall. The children crowded round eagerly. They saw rough steps hewn in the rock – and they could see that the seaweed that grew around had been bruised and torn.

'See that seaweed?' said Jack excitedly. 'Well, somebody has trodden on that! That's the way – up there! Come on, everybody!'

With their torches flashing the children tried to climb up the steep rocky steps in the cave-wall. They were slippery, and it was very difficult.

Suddenly Peggy caught sight of something that looked like a black worm hanging down the wall, and she shone her torch on it.

'Here's a rope!' she said. 'Look! Look! It must be to pull ourselves up by!'

The others stared at the rope. Mike caught hold of it. It hung down from a black hole at the top of the rocky wall, and as he pulled it, it held firm.

'Yes, that's what it is!' said Mike. 'It's fastened to something overhead, and is meant to help anyone using this cave. I'll go up first with the rope's help, and you others can follow.'

It was easy to get up the slippery, rocky steps with the rope to help them. Mike swung himself through the dark opening at the top of the sloping wall. He shone his torch around.

He was in another cave, but much smaller. A few boxes and barrels lay around, empty and half broken.

Mike called down excitedly. 'This has been used by smugglers in the olden days! There are still the old boxes here that must have brought the brandy and silks and things that the smugglers hid. Come along, you others!'

One by one they scrambled up. Jack kicked the boxes. They were all empty. 'Unpacked by smugglers years and years ago!' said Jack. He shone his torch round the cave. 'Where do we go from here?' he wondered. 'Ah, look – is that a door or something over there?'

'Yes,' said Mike, who was nearest. 'A good solid oak door too, fitted with bolts! I say, what a shame if it's locked.'

He tried it – but it was not locked. It swung heavily into the cave, showing beyond it a narrow passage cut out of the rock itself.

'*Here's* the passage!' cried Mike, in the greatest excitement. 'I say! Isn't this thrilling?'

'Mike, don't make such a row,' said Jack. 'We don't know if anyone is coming down the passage or not, and if they should be, they'll hear us easily! Let me go first. My torch is the brightest.'

He went up the dark, damp passage. It was so low in places that the children had to put down their heads in case they were bumped. The passage wound round and round and in and out, always going uphill, sometimes quite steeply. After a while it was not cut out of the rock, but out of sand and soil. It was quite dry by the time they had gone a few hundred yards.

Except for the noise that their feet made now and again the children were perfectly quiet. Presently they came to a wider piece of the passage and this widened out so much in a few moments that it became a kind of underground room. Here were more boxes, larger ones and much stronger looking. All were empty.

'Think of the old-time smugglers sitting here and having a feast, opening the boxes and barrels, selling the goods, going off again in the middle of the night!' said Peggy, looking round. The children could imagine it all very well.

'Aren't we nearly up to the Old House now, Jack?'

asked Nora. 'We seem to have come a long way, always going uphill!'

'I think we must be very near,' said Jack, in a low voice. 'That oak door over there in the corner must lead into the cellars, I should think.'

'Let's open it and see,' whispered Mike. He took hold of the iron handle of the door and pushed gently. It opened outwards, and Mike looked through it. There was a flight of stone steps beyond, leading steeply upwards.

The children went softly up them. There were eighteen of them.

At the top Jack swung his torch around. They were in a dark, underground cellar, set round with shelves. Empty bottles stood in rows. Barrels stood in corners.

'This is the cellar of the Old House, I'm sure,' said Jack. 'And look – there are the steps leading into the house itself!'

His torch showed a short flight of steps in the far corner, leading up to a door that stood ajar, for a faint crack of daylight came through.

'You stay here, and I'll slip up and see if I can hear anything,' said Jack. The others stayed as still as mice. Jack went quietly up the steps. He swung the door a little farther open and listened.

He could hear nothing. He peeped through the door. A large stone-floored scullery lay beyond the door. Nobody seemed about at all. Jack tried to remember where the tower would be. Of course! It would be quite near the scullery – maybe a door would lead from the scullery into the tower, so that servants could take the meals there when necessary.

Jack slipped through the door and took a quick look round. Yes – there was a little stout door at the end of the big scullery, just like the door through which the children had gone into the tower! It must lead there.

Now that he had gone so far Jack felt as if he must go farther! He tiptoed through the scullery, and tried the little tower door. It opened! He slipped through and ran up the winding stairs of the tower. He went right to the top – and when he got there he stopped in amazement.

He could hear somebody crying inside the top room of the tower. It sounded like a child. Jack tried the door – but alas, that was locked! He knocked softly.

The person inside stopped crying at once. 'Who is it?' said a voice.

But just as Jack was going to answer, he heard the sound of voices. Someone was coming up the tower stairs! What was Jack to do? He couldn't hide in the room at the top! But perhaps there was time to hide in the room below – if only they didn't come there!

He slipped quickly down the stairs and into the room below, which was roughly furnished with a rug and a chair and table. Jack hid behind the door.

The voices came nearer as the people came up the winding staircase. Jack trembled with excitement behind the door.

The footsteps stopped outside the room where Jack was hiding. 'I'll just see if I left my papers in here,' said the voice of sleepy-eyed Luiz. The door was pushed open a little farther, and Luiz looked in!

# A Narrow Escape!

Jack was quite sure that Luiz would see him when he popped his head in by the door. His heart beat so loudly that he thought Luiz would hear it. But to his great astonishment and joy Luiz glanced over to the table by the window, and then shut the door and went on up the tower stairs.

'My papers are not there,' Jack heard him say to his companion. The boy could hardly believe that he had not been seen. He waited until he heard the door of the room above unlocked, and then he quietly opened his own door, shot down the stairs at top speed, ran through the little door into the scullery and down the cellar steps, falling in a heap at the bottom.

'Jack!' whispered Mike in surprise. 'What's the matter? What a long time you've been!'

'I was nearly caught!' said Jack, panting. 'Tell you all about it in a minute. Let's get out of this cellar down into that underground room. Hurry!'

They all climbed down the eighteen steps to the underground room. They were longing to know what had happened to Jack.

'Let's sit down here for a minute,' said Jack. They sat down on the old boxes and barrels. 'I'll tell you what happened,' said Jack. 'I tiptoed through the scullery to the door that leads into the tower from here – and slipped up the winding staircase to the top – but the top door was locked. *And there was somebody crying behind it*!'

'Crying!' said Nora, in surprise. 'Is there a prisoner in the tower, then?'

'Must be,' said Jack. 'And it sounds like a boy or a girl, too! Isn't it mysterious?'

'Perhaps they're not smuggling silks and things, then, but have got a prisoner,' said Peggy seriously. 'Perhaps it was the prisoner they brought in last night by that motor-boat and took through the secret passage to the tower.'

'I think you're right, Peggy,' said Jack. 'Now we'll have to find out *somehow* who it is!'

'Well, I should think the prisoner will look out of the tower window sometime!' said Nora. 'We could borrow Dimmy's field-glasses and keep a watch, couldn't we? Then we should see what sort of a prisoner it is.'

'Good idea, Nora,' said Mike. 'We could easily take it in turns to keep watch for that.'

'I feel jolly hungry,' said Peggy. 'Isn't it about time we had our lunch? All this exploring has taken ages. What's the time, Jack?'

Jack looked at his watch. 'It's getting late,' he said. 'We'll go back to the beach and eat our lunch there. Come on! We don't want to eat in this dark, dismal room!'

They went back to the secret passage. It was easier going down it than up. Bending their heads down every now and again the children made their way down it, stumbling over the rough, rocky path underfoot. Nora's torch had no more light showing in it, so she walked close behind Jack, trying to see by the light of his.

At last they came to the cave that was over the shore cave. The rope hung down through the hole that led to the steps down the cave-wall. Jack got hold of it. He began to climb down – but he hadn't gone far before he gave a shout of dismay.

'I say! What do you think's happened?'

'What?' cried everyone anxiously.

'Why, the tide's come in whilst we've been exploring, and the shore cave is full of water!' shouted Jack. 'It's almost up to the roof of the cave. We can't possibly get down this way.'

He climbed back into the cave above. The children looked at each other gloomily by the light of their torches.

'What idiots we are!' said Mike. 'We never thought about the tide. If we *had* thought we'd have known it was coming in and that we'd be nicely caught by it. It won't be out of this cave for ages.'

'What are we going to do?' said Nora. 'I'm so hungry. Can't we eat our lunch now?'

'It's damp and cold here,' said Jack, with a shiver. 'We shall all get chills if we sit in this cave. We'd better go back to that underground room. At least it's dry there. We can light our candles and eat our food by their light. Our torches won't last much longer if we use them such a lot.'

So back they toiled up the secret passage till they came to the underground room. And there, where many a time the smugglers had sat and feasted and smoked, the four children undid their kit-bags and took out all the delicious things that Dimmy had put in for them.

Veal and ham pies had never tasted quite so good! And as for the ginger cake, the children could have done with twice as much! They finished up every scrap of everything, hard-boiled eggs and all, and then drank the sweet lemonade.

'That's better,' said Jack, grinning round at the others by the light of four shining candles. 'I *was* hungry.'

Mike looked at his watch. 'It's four o'clock,' he said. 'I don't suppose that cave will be clear till at least half-past five – and even then the beach is washed by huge waves that might sweep us off our feet. What a bore!'

'I'm simply longing to have a look at the tower of the Old House from the window of *our* tower,' said Nora. 'I do want to see who the prisoner is. Wouldn't it be lovely if we could rescue him!'

'Jack, couldn't we escape through the grounds straightaway now?' said Peggy. 'If we went up into the cellars again, and into the scullery, and down the tradesmen's entrance to the back gate we could easily get home in ten minutes – instead of waiting for hours for the tide to go out of the cave!'

'Well, we'll have to be jolly careful,' said Jack, who also didn't want to wait for hours for the tide. 'I'll go first as usual and see that all's clear.'

They all went up the eighteen steps into the cellar. Jack slipped up the steps to the scullery. No one was there. He could hear voices in the kitchen, but he guessed that the maids there were having their tea.

Everything was quiet. Jack gave a low whistle and the others came up the steps quietly. They tiptoed to the back door, where a row of empty milk bottles stood, waiting for the milkman.

And then they saw something that filled them with dismay! Two big Airedale dogs were roaming about the garden!

'Look!' whispered Jack. 'They'll never let us pass. I'd forgotten that they'd got dogs to guard the place.'

Nora looked as if she were going to cry. First it was the tide that stopped them – and now it was two dogs.

'Do you think they'd hurt us if we tried to slip out of the grounds?' said Peggy.

'No,' said Jack, 'but they'd bark the place down, and we'd be found at once. Wait a minute whilst I think what to do.'

'Ay, ay, Captain!' said Mike. The others waited obediently. Jack was always good at thinking of ideas when they were in a fix.

'I know what,' said Jack at last. 'We'll go into this little wash-house here and hide behind that heap of sacks. They *must* call in the dogs when a tradesman comes, or they wouldn't get any goods. Well, we'll wait till someone comes – the milkman or the baker – and as soon as the dogs are called in, we will slip out! We won't go down the back path, we'll make for that tree over there and climb it. I believe we could drop on to the top of the wall from its branches and get down the other side quite safely.'

'Good idea!' said Mike. They all crouched down in the little wash-house, first of all shutting the door so that no dog could wander inside and find them.

They waited. Jack sometimes popped his head up and peeped out of the window, but no one came. Then they heard the rattling of the milkman's van down the lane and Jack grinned at the others.

'Be ready,' he whispered. The milkman got down from his van and rang a bell at the back gate. At once the two dogs set up a terrific barking. Luiz appeared round the house and called them. He tied the dogs to a tree and shouted to the milkman.

'All right! The dogs are tied. You can come in.'

The milkman went up the path with some bottles and some butter. A voice came from the kitchen. 'Come right in, please.' He disappeared inside the scullery.

'Now's our chance!' whispered Jack. 'Luiz is gone. The dogs are tied. Run!'

The four of them ran through the wash-house door and sprinted across the grass to the tree that Jack had pointed out. The dogs saw them and began barking again, pulling at their leads as if they would break them.

'Lie down and be quiet!' yelled a voice from somewhere around the house. The dogs went on barking – but in a minute or two the children were safely up the tree, hidden in the branches. Still the dogs went on barking and barking.

Luiz appeared again, and shouted at them. 'Quiet, I tell you!' he yelled. 'It's only the milkman!'

But the dogs knew that it wasn't and they barked till they were hoarse. The children waited till Luiz had gone again and then one by one they climbed from a branch to the top of the wall, and dropped down to the other side in safety.

How glad they were! How they tore down the slope

to Peep-Hole, giggling as they went. What an adventure they had had!

'Secret caves and passages, and finding a prisoner, and nearly getting caught ourselves!' panted Mike, as they reached Peep-Hole. 'It's all too exciting for anything!'

'And now we've got to find out *who* the poor prisoner is,' said Nora. 'That's what *I'm* longing to know!'

Dimmy met them in the hall. 'So you're back again,' she said. 'Did you have a good picnic? What a lovely sunny day it has been, hasn't it?'

'Has it?' said the children, trying to remember – but all they could remember was darkness and dampness in the secret passage and caves and cellar! 'We really didn't notice if the weather was sunny or not, Dimmy!'

'What nonsense you do talk!' said Dimmy. 'Go and get ready for tea. I've got you the last of the big red eating gooseberries out of the garden!'

'Good old Dimmy-Duck!' yelled Mike, and he tore upstairs to wash – but before he washed he went to his window to look across at the tower window of the Old House. When would he see somebody looking out there?

# The Prisoner in the Tower

The four children were in a great state of excitement. They could talk about nothing else but the secret passage and the prisoner in the tower, though when Dimmy was there they had to stop, and talk of other things.

'We simply *must* keep it all a secret,' said Mike. 'I'm quite sure Dimmy would be worried. The only thing I'm wondering about is – how are we going to keep a watch on the tower of the Old House in the daytime, without Dimmy wondering what we are doing? It was easy enough at night – but in the daytime it won't be so easy.'

'Well, we'll *have* to be out of our rooms whilst Dimmy is cleaning them each day,' said Peggy. 'But as soon as the cleaning is done we could take it in turns to go into the top bedroom and watch, without Dimmy knowing. We could have fairly long watches – say three hours. We needn't keep our eyes on the tower *all* the time – we could read or something and keep looking up. I shall do my knitting.'

'And I shall do my jigsaw,' said Mike. I can do that and keep looking up easily.'

'We'll begin tomorrow morning,' said Jack. 'I hope Dimmy doesn't go up to our bedroom and find one of us there – she'll think we've quarrelled or something!'

They took a look at the tower in the distance as they went to bed that night. But there was nothing to be seen. Nobody looked out. A dim light shone, that was all.

'There must be somebody there *now*,' said Jack. 'Or they wouldn't have a light. Goodness, I'm sure I shall never go to sleep tonight! My mind keeps thinking of secret caves!'

They did lie awake rather a long time, but at last they were all asleep and dreaming. They dreamt of caves and passages and towers and prisoners, and had just as exciting a time in their sleep as they had had in the daytime.

Mike looked at the distant tower as soon as he jumped out of bed next morning, but there was no one there. Jack took a glance as he was about to go downstairs – and he gave a cry.

'There's someone at the window!'

Mike came rushing to see – but Jack pushed him back. 'Don't go too near our window. If we can see them they can see us – and it looks to me as if it's only Mr Diaz.'

The two boys kept back a little so that no one could see them. Yes – it *was* Mr Diaz – and he was looking straight at their window.

'Keep quite still, Mike,' he said. 'He's just trying to find out how much we can see of his tower, I'm sure!'

Mr Diaz drew back after a while. Dimmy rang the breakfast bell again downstairs, and Peggy came bounding up the winding staircase to find out what the boys were doing.

That day the children began their three-hourly

watches – and it was just as Peggy was taking over from Jack about six o'clock that evening that they first saw the Prisoner!

Jack had been carving a wooden boat with his penknife, sitting patiently for three hours at one side of the window so that Mr Diaz would not catch sight of him if he should happen to look out once more. Every minute or two Jack glanced over to the distant tower, but he had seen no one there.

Then Peggy came running up the stairs to take her turn at watching – and just as Jack was getting up from his chair, and Peggy was picking up her knitting, they both happened to glance at the far window.

And they both saw the same thing!

'It's a little boy!' said Jack, in the greatest astonishment. 'He doesn't look more than seven or eight!'

'He doesn't look English,' said Peggy. 'Even from here he looks very dark-haired and dark-eyed.'

The little boy in the distant tower leaned on the windowsill. Jack took up the field-glasses that lay near at hand and looked through them. He could then see the little boy looking as near as if he were in the garden of Peep-Hole!

'He looks awfully pale and miserable,' said Jack. 'Almost as if he were crying!'

'Let *me* see,' said Peggy. Jack gave her the glasses. She looked through them. 'Yes,' she said. 'He certainly does look sad. I'm not surprised, either, if he's a prisoner!'

'Let's wave to him!' said Jack suddenly. 'He'll be glad to see other children.' Jack leaned right out of his window, and began waving violently.

At first the boy in the tower did not notice. Then Jack's moving arm attracted his attention, and he stared. Jack almost fell out of the window, because he waved so hard. Peggy squeezed beside him and waved too. The boy smiled and waved back. First he put one hand out of the window and then both, and waved them like flags!

'Good! He's seen us,' said Jack, pleased. 'Now the next thing is – how are we going to find out who he is?'

Peggy had a good idea. 'If we did some big letters in black ink, and held them up at the window one after the other, to spell out words, he would know we were friends!'

'Good idea!' said Jack. 'It looks as if it's going to be rainy tonight, so we could all come up here and do the letters then. Dimmy's got a friend coming in to see her, I know, so she won't mind us coming up here.'

'I wonder if she's got some black ink,' said Peggy. 'We'll ask her. I've got some sheets of drawing paper we can use.'

The little boy at the tower window suddenly disappeared and did not come back. 'I expect somebody came into the tower room, and he came away from the window in case they guessed that he was signalling to someone,' said Jack.

Mike and Nora came running in through the garden at that moment, for it was raining. They rushed up to the bedroom at the top of their tower to see why Jack hadn't come down to the beach.

When they heard about the boy prisoner in the tower of the Old House, they wished that they had seen him

71

too. They were thrilled when Jack told them that they were all going to make giant black letters so that they might spell out words to the prisoner.

Peggy ran to see if Dimmy had any black ink, but she hadn't.

'I've only the ordinary blue ink,' said Dimmy, rummaging in her desk. 'But look – here's some black charcoal. Will that do instead?'

'Oh yes!' cried Peggy. 'Thank you, Dimmy. You won't mind if we all play in Mike's bedroom this evening, will you? You are having a friend to keep you company, aren't you?'

'Oh yes,' said Dimmy. 'I'll be glad to have you four monkeys out of my way! You do what you like up there, but have the windows open so that you get plenty of fresh air.'

'Oh, we'll be very particular about the windows, Dimmy!' said Peggy, laughing, and she ran off with the box of black charcoal.

She took the big white drawing sheets from her box, and went up to Mike's bedroom. She gave some to each of the children, and opened the box of black charcoal.

'We *shall* make our hands black!' she said. 'Isn't the charcoal nice and black, Mike? The letters we make will show up well, and the prisoner will easily be able to read them.'

'Make them about a foot and a half tall and as thick as you can,' said Jack, sketching out a big letter A. 'I'll do the first six letters, you do the next six, Mike, Peggy the next six, and Nora the next. Whoever has finished first can do the odd two letters left. Look at my big A! I guess the prisoner could easily see that from his window.'

It was indeed a big A, nearly as high as the stool on which Jack was sitting. It was thickly done too, and surely anybody would be able to read it from quite a distance.

It did not take the children very long to finish all the letters. Peggy had done hers first, so she did Y and Z too, though she was sure they would not want to use the Z.

They had kept their eye on the tower window, but the boy had not appeared again. Now, with the rainy sky, the dark was coming down. A faint light appeared in the distant tower window. For a moment the children saw the outline of a boy's head and shoulders at the window, and then it was gone again.

'We can't do any signalling till tomorrow,' said Jack. 'What a pity! All the letters are ready!'

Again the next day the children kept a three-hourly watch, and about two o'clock in the afternoon Jack and Nora saw the boy prisoner. He came to the window and leaned out as far as he could.

'He's looking down into the grounds to make sure that nobody can see him waving to us,' said Jack. 'Sensible fellow!'

Jack waved from his window, and the boy saw him and waved back. 'Now we'll do a bit of letter-work!' said Jack excitedly. 'Give me the letters I want, Nora, please, and I'll send him a message. I hope he can read!'

'What message are you sending?' asked Nora.

'Well, I think I'll just say, "WE ARE FRIENDS",' said Jack. 'Hand me the letters one by one.'

So Nora handed Jack the big letters drawn in black on the white paper. First a big W, then a big E, and so on. The boy prisoner watched the letters eagerly.

He read the words as the letters made them and nodded his head and smiled and waved. Then he began making letters with his fingers – but Jack could not see them so far away. He snatched up the field-glasses and looked through them. The boy began his message again. He held up one finger first.

'That's "I",' said Jack. Then the boy slanted his two fingers together and crossed them with a middle finger.

'That's "A",' said Jack. Then the boy turned his hands the other way and made the letter M with four fingers.

'"M"!' said Jack. '"I AM" he has spelt out so far, Nora.'

The boy went on making the letters very cleverly with his fingers – and he spelt out the message 'I AM A PRISONER.'

By this time Mike and Peggy had come upstairs to get their swimsuits, which they had forgotten – but when they saw what was going on they sat down excitedly on Mike's bed, whilst Jack spelt out the prisoner's message.

'Jack, ask him who he is!' cried Nora, dancing up and down in excitement. So Jack spelt out the question with his black letters. And, dear me, *what* a surprising answer he got!

# The Rope Ladder

Jack had been watching the boy's answer through the field-glasses. The others sat near him, waiting eagerly to know who the boy was. They could see him making letters with his fingers, but they could not see what letters they were for, unlike Jack, they had no glasses to help them.

'Who is he, Jack? Who is the prisoner?' cried Nora impatiently.

'Well,' said Jack, turning to them, 'he has just spelt out on his fingers that he is Prince Paul!'

The others stared at him in surprise.

'Prince Paul!' said Peggy. 'A prince! What country is he prince of?'

'I don't know,' said Jack. 'I'll ask him. Where are the letters?'

But by the time he had got the first one, Prince Paul had disappeared. He went quite suddenly, as if someone had pulled him back. Jack darted back from his own window, and pulled Peggy with him. They almost fell on the floor and Peggy was quite cross.

'Don't, Jack,' she began – but then she saw Jack's face, and she followed his eyes, and saw what he saw. Mr Diaz and sleepy-eyed Luiz were both at the far tower window – and they were looking very hard indeed at the children's window.

'Did he see us, Jack?' said Peggy, speaking in a whisper, as if she was afraid that Mr Diaz might hear her.

'No,' said Jack. 'We got away just in time. Maybe they went into the prisoner's room and caught him signalling. Or maybe they just took him away from the window because they wanted to look out themselves. I'm sure they know this is our bedroom!'

'Jack, do you think we can possibly rescue that boy?' asked Nora eagerly. 'And do you think he really is a prince?'

'We can't rescue him by using the secret passage,' said Jack, 'because even if we used it, it only takes us to the cellars, and Mr Diaz keeps the tower-room locked. This is going to be difficult.'

'We shall have to be very careful not to be seen by Mr Diaz at our window,' said Nora. 'Perhaps he already thinks we know about the prisoner.'

'He can't know that,' said Jack. 'He didn't see our messages.'

'I say! I've got an idea!' said Mike. 'What about us making a rope ladder and getting up to the tower-room on it at night?'

'But how could we get it up to the window?' said Nora.

'Well, if we can tell the prisoner about it he can help to pull it up,' said Jack. 'You know how to get a rope ladder up to a high window, don't you? First of all you tie a stone or something heavy on to a long piece of string. Then you tie the piece of string on to a thin twine. Then you tie the twine to the rope ladder. You throw the stone up to the window and the person there catches it, pulls up the string, pulls up the twine – and the rope ladder comes last of all! He fixes it safely to something and escapes!'

'That's a *great* idea!' said the others.

'Let's try it,' said Peggy.

'We'll have to get string and twine and rope,' said Nora.

'George will let us have some,' said Mike.

'Let's go and ask him now!' said Jack, jumping up. So down the stairs they rushed and out into the field where they knew George was working that day.

'George, George! Can you let us have lots of string and twine and rope?' yelled Jack.

'I dare say,' said George. 'What do you want it for?'

'It's a secret,' said Mike. 'We'll tell you later on.'

'You can go to my old boat in the cove and open the locker there,' said George. 'There's a mighty lot of string and stuff all tangled up there. You can have the loan of it if you want it.'

'Oh, thank you, George!' cried the four children, and they tore off to the cove. They found George's boat and opened the locker at one end of it. Sure enough there *was* a mighty lot of string and twine and rope there, that George used for mending and making fishing-nets.

'Goodness! It'll take some time to untangle all this!' said Peggy.

'Well, there's four of us to do it,' said Jack. 'We might as well sit here in the boat and get on with it now.'

'What shall we make the rungs of the ladder with?' said Peggy.

'There's some little wooden stakes, quite strong, in Dimmy's garden shed,' said Jack. 'I saw them there the other day. They would be the very thing!'

'Look! Look!' said Peggy suddenly, in a low voice. The others looked up, and saw, coming across the sand towards them, the yellow-haired woman who had been with Mr Diaz in the car, and who lived at the Old House.

'That must be Mrs Diaz,' said Nora. 'Is she coming to talk to us, I wonder?'

'Leave *me* to do the talking,' said Jack. 'She's been sent to find out how much we know, I'm sure.'

Mrs Diaz came slowly over to them, holding a big sunshade over her head. She nodded to the children.

'You are very busy,' she said. 'What are you doing?'

'Oh, playing about in George's boat,' said Jack.

'You are often on the beach?' asked the woman, putting down her sunshade. 'You play all the time here?'

'Nearly all,' said Jack. 'We can't when the tide is in.'

'Have you seen these exciting caves?' asked Mrs Diaz, pointing to the caves with her sunshade. 'Have you ever been in any, I wonder?'

'We don't like them because they are dark and damp,' said Jack.

'Have none of the other children any tongues?' asked Mrs Diaz, in a slightly sharp voice.

'They're rather shy,' said Jack. 'I'm their captain, anyway, so I do the talking.'

'Oh,' said Mrs Diaz. She made a pattern in the sand with her sunshade point. 'How long are you staying at Peep-Hole?' she asked.

'Oh, not long,' said Jack.

'Your bedrooms are in the tower, aren't they?' asked Mrs Diaz, looking straight at Jack. Jack looked straight back.

'Yes,' he said. They are.'

'Can you see the Old House from your bedrooms?' asked the golden-haired woman.

'I'll look and see when we get back tonight,' answered Jack.

Just then the children heard the sound of Dimmy's

tea-bell and they scrambled up, glad to be able to get away from the strange woman's questions. Mike took a bundle of the rope with him, meaning to go on with the untangling of it at Peep-Hole. But Jack signalled quietly to him to leave it, so he put it down.

'Goodbye,' said the children politely, and ran over the sands at top speed.

'Jack, you *were* clever at answering those awkward questions of hers!' panted Mike. 'I don't know *what* I would have said if she had asked *me* if I could see the Old House from our bedroom window!'

'Jack said he'd look and see when we got back tonight!' giggled Peggy. 'How *did* you think of that answer, Jack?'

'You know, they suspect us of knowing about their prisoner,' said Jack. 'They'll be on the look-out now, more than ever. I guess we shan't be able to do much more signalling to the prisoner boy.'

'Why did you make me leave the bundle of rope behind?' asked Mike. 'I thought if I took it with me that we could undo it and get on with the ladder here in our bedroom, after tea.'

'But, Mike, Mrs Diaz is sure to guess we're up to something if you go lugging bundles of rope about,' said Jack. 'We'd far better go back and get it after tea.'

'You're right as usual, Captain,' said Mike.

So after tea they went back to the boat to get the rope, and took it up to their room. The tide was in and there was nothing to do on the beach. It would be fun to make the ladder.

'What *are* you all doing up there?' called Dimmy, in

surprise. 'Aren't you going out this evening?'

'No, Dimmy. We've got a secret on,' called back Nora. 'You don't mind, do you?'

'Not a bit!' said Dimmy, and went back to her washing-up. The children worked hard at the rope. Soon they had a great deal of it untangled, and they found that it was good strong rope, knotted here and there. They chose two long lengths, and then Mike went down to get the little stakes from the shed. He soon came back with them. Jack showed the others how to knot the ends of the stakes firmly to the sides of the rope ladder. The stakes were the rungs. Soon the ladder took shape under their hands.

'Doesn't it look fine!' cried Peggy. 'I'm simply *longing* to use it! Do let's use it tonight, Jack!'

# Jack Has an Adventure

'We can't possibly use the rope ladder tonight to rescue Prince Paul,' said Jack. 'For one thing, there are those fierce dogs. They would never let us get into the grounds at night. They would bark the place down.'

'Gracious! I forgot the dogs!' said Nora in dismay. 'What can we do, then?'

'The only thing to do is to make friends with the dogs,' said Jack.

The other three stared at him. None of them felt that they wanted to make friends with the two big dogs. Jack grinned.

'Don't look so scared,' he said. '*I'll* be the one to make friends. Animals are good with me. Until I met you and came to live with you I lived on a farm, and I know all about animals and their ways.'

'Oh, Jack!' said Nora. 'You're marvellous! Will you really make friends with those dogs?'

'It's the only thing to do,' said Jack. 'And I'm going to begin tonight. As soon as those dogs will let me pass in as a friend, I'll be able to take the rope ladder in some night and get Prince Paul down.'

'How are you going to make friends?' asked Mike.

'I'll get some meat and biscuits from Dimmy,' said Jack.

'She *will* think you're hungry all of a sudden,' said Mike with a grin.

Dimmy was surprised to hear that Jack wanted some meat and biscuits that evening. She had given the children a good supper of stewed raspberries, cream, and home-made bread and butter, and as Jack had had three helpings she really couldn't believe that he now wanted meat and biscuits.

'I think you must be going to have a midnight feast in your room,' she said. 'Well – for once in a way I'll let you have it.'

Jack chuckled, and winked at the others. 'It's for a midnight picnic all right!' he said. 'But not in my bedroom, Dimmy.'

Dimmy didn't hear the last bit, for she had gone out of the room. She made Jack some ham sandwiches and gave him a bag of biscuits. He was pleased.

'Thank you,' he said. 'That's jolly good of you, Dimmy.'

'Well, if you feel ill tomorrow, it'll be your own fault,' said Dimmy, with a laugh. She really was an awfully good sort.

When it got dark Jack put the sandwiches and biscuits into a bag and said goodbye to the others. They wanted to come too and wait outside the wall, but Jack wouldn't let them.

'No,' he said. 'If they smell you or hear you those dogs will bark their heads off. I must go alone. I'll come back in about two hours.'

He slipped down the winding staircase and out into the garden without Dimmy seeing him. He set off quietly up the cliff towards the Old House, which loomed up large and dark against the night sky. He could quite well see the round tower on one side of it, and at the top was a faint light.

'I suppose poor Prince Paul is up there trying to read or something,' said Jack to himself, feeling sorry for the little prisoner all alone in the tall tower. 'How I wish we could rescue him quickly!'

He soon came to the wall. He wondered how to slip into the grounds without making the dogs bark too loudly. They were always loose at night and might come rushing at him if he went in by the gate.

And then a lucky thing happened. One of the maids came up the lane and turned in at the back gate, quite near to where Jack stood. At once the two dogs rushed up and began to bark madly at the woman.

She was used to them, however, and spoke sharply. 'Don! Tinker! Be quiet! Don't you know me yet?'

A voice called from the house. 'Is that you, Anna?'

'Yes, sir,' answered the woman. 'It's only me they're barking at.'

'That was Mr Diaz's voice,' said Jack to himself. 'Now's my chance. If I slip in now and the dogs go on barking, Mr Diaz will simply think it's because of Anna. And maybe I can make them stop barking in a little while.'

He slid in silently at the back gate like a black shadow. Both the dogs heard him and smelt him, and set up a great barking again.

'Quiet!' roared Mr Diaz. 'Quiet!'

The dogs paused in their barking. Mr Diaz only said 'Quiet!' when the visitor was a friend. The pause was enough for Jack.

'Don! Tinker!' he said in a low voice, and then he sat himself down on the ground beside a thick bush. The dogs heard their names and pricked up their ears. Don barked loudly again. Tinker looked as if he wanted to rush at Jack – but this boy was sitting down like a friend! It was strange!

Jack made no movement. He knew from his life on the farm that animals and birds are afraid of sudden quick movements, even from a friend. His heart beat loudly, for he was not at all sure that one or both of the dogs might not attack him.

Don barked again. Tinker ran up to Jack and sniffed at him. Jack sat perfectly still. The dog smelt the meat sandwiches and the biscuits and tried to get his nose in the bag. Both dogs were underfed, because Mr Diaz thought they would be wide awake then, if they were hungry, and would not sleep as well as a properly fed dog does.

'Good dog, Tinker, good dog,' said Jack in a very low

voice. The dog sniffed hungrily at the bag. Jack slowly and cautiously undid it. Don, the other dog, would not come near. He stood at a distance, very suspicious, growling softly.

'Growl all you like!' thought Jack. 'But don't start that dreadful barking again. I don't want Mr Diaz out here looking round!'

Tinker took a ham sandwich from Jack's hand. It was gone at a gulp, for the dog was very hungry indeed. He sniffed for another.

Jack slowly put out his hand to the dog's head and patted it gently. The dog was not used to being kindly treated and was surprised. He gave Jack's hand a quick lick.

'We're getting on!' thought the boy. He gave Tinker another sandwich, and that was swallowed at once. Don smelt the meat from where he stood. He decided that if Tinker was friendly to this strange boy, he could be too – and also he badly wanted that nice-smelling meat.

So he ran up, still growling softly. But Jack knew it was a pretend-growl, and he chuckled to himself. He gave the hungry animal a sandwich, and then another. The dog swallowed them both. There were only two more left, so Jack gave the dogs one each.

Then he stood up and took a few cautious steps towards the tower. The dogs did not seem to mind. They could now smell Jack's biscuits and they kept close to the boy as he walked. Tinker was very friendly indeed, and licked Jack's hand when he found it near his nose. Don would not do that, but he no longer growled.

Jack walked to the foot of the tower and looked up. He gave each dog a biscuit, and wondered if by any chance the door at the foot of the tower was unlocked. If it was, dare he run up the winding stairway and try to talk to the prisoner? Maybe he could even unlock the door and get the boy out? But no – the dogs would not know Prince Paul and might bark and then they would both be caught.

He tried the door. It opened! Jack listened. No one seemed to be about at all. The dogs pressed against him, asking for another biscuit. He threw them each one a little way off and then slipped through the door leaving it open.

The dogs ate the biscuits, and then lay down by the door to wait for this unexpected friend to come back. They hoped he would have some more biscuits!

Jack stood at the bottom of the tower stairway and listened. The stone steps were dark. Not a sound was to be heard. Jack got out his torch and switched it on. Then, making no sound, the brave boy slowly went up the steps, only using his torch at the awkward parts, for he was afraid of slipping there and making a noise.

There were no lights in the rooms he passed. Only when he came to the top room did he see a streak of light under the door. He stood outside and listened. Somebody was crying inside. Jack looked for the keyhole and put his eye to it.

He could see a small boy sitting at a table with his head on his hands. He was crying quietly, and the tears fell on to a page of the book in front of him. Nobody else seemed to be in the room as far as Jack could see or hear.

Jack knocked very gently on the door. The boy inside raised his head.

'Who is there?' he asked.

'It's Jack, one of your friends!' answered Jack in a low tone. 'I'm one of the children you've seen waving to you in the tower. I've made friends with the two dogs and I've slipped up here to talk to you.'

'Oh!' cried the boy, in a voice of great delight. 'Can you let me out? Is the door locked on the outside? See if they have left the key.'

Jack felt. He tried the door. It was locked and bolted. He could undo the bolts easily enough – but there was no key to unlock the door. It was hopeless.

'I can't rescue you tonight,' said Jack. 'But listen, please. We've made a rope ladder that will reach your window. If you hear a stone rattling up one night that falls into your room, pick it up at once. It will be tied to a string. Pull the string, and some twine will come up. Pull the twine and it will bring up the rope ladder. See? Fix the ladder to something and get down it.'

'Oh, thank you!' said the boy. He pressed his face to

the door and Jack could hear him sigh. 'I am so tired of being shut up here.'

'Why are you a prisoner?' asked Jack.

'It is a long story,' said the boy. 'My father is King of Baronia, and he is ill. If he dies, I shall be king – and my uncle does not want me to be. So he has paid some men to kidnap me and carry me away. Then, if my father dies and I am not there to become king, my uncle will seize the throne and make himself king before I can be found!'

'So you really *are* a prince!' said Jack. 'We wondered *if* you were. What a wicked shame to keep you prisoner like this! Shall we tell the police, Paul?'

'Oh no,' said Paul at once. 'If Mr Diaz and Luiz think that the police know about me they might harm me in some way – and certainly they would smuggle me down that secret passage and then you would never know where I had gone. Please try to rescue me yourself. What is your name?'

'I'm Jack,' said Jack. 'Look here, Prince, keep your eyes open for our letter-messages from our tower. We will let you know when we are coming at night with the rope ladder.'

'You are very good,' said the little prince. 'I was so pleased when I saw you waving.'

'I must go,' said Jack. 'I think I can hear something. I mustn't be caught. Goodbye!'

He slipped down the stairs, and tried to open the tower door – but it was now locked! Mr Diaz had been along, found it open, and had locked it, although he had no idea that Jack was inside.

Jack stood inside the locked door, with his heart beating loudly. How could he get out? Perhaps the kitchen door could be opened without noise?

He went to the door that led from the tower to the scullery. There was no sound to be heard beyond it. Jack opened it cautiously. He stepped into the big, dark scullery, meaning to creep across to the back door, open it and escape through the grounds.

But, alas for Jack! He walked straight into a tin bath, and fell over it with a most tremendous clatter!

# Another Narrow Escape

Jack picked himself up at once in a fright. The door into the scullery opened, and Anna looked in, switching on the light. She screamed when she saw Jack, and ran back into the kitchen, shouting for Luiz.

'Luiz! Luiz! There is a burglar in the scullery!'

Jack ran to the back door and tried to open it. But it was locked and bolted and even had a chain on it, too. The boy knew quite well that by the time he had undone everything he would be caught! He was in despair. Whatever could he do? It was no use to run back up the stairs to the tower-rooms, for he would be caught there too.

And then he thought of something. Of course! He could escape down the secret passage! He had his torch with him, and he could easily see the way.

He ran to the cellar door. Fortunately that was open. He leapt down the steps into the cellar just as Mr Diaz and Luiz came tearing into the kitchen. He heard them shouting, 'Where is he? Where is he?'

Jack sped to the eighteen stone steps that led down to the door of the underground room. He ran down them, using his torch. He opened the thick door at the bottom. He ran through the large underground room there to the secret passage.

His heart was beating fast and his breath was coming in pants. He made his way down the secret passage, bending his head every now and again when he came to the narrow, low parts. Soon he came to the damp piece, and knew that he would presently come to the small cave that lay above the large shore cave.

He came to the oak door that led into the small cave. He pushed it open and made his way to where he knew the rope hung to help him down into the big beach cave.

'Then all I'll have to do is to slip round the sands, up the cliff path and into Peep-Hole,' thought the boy thankfully.

But what a dreadful shock for Jack – once more the tide was in and the water filled the big cave. He could not possibly get home that way. He would have to wait till it went out.

'I only hope that they don't realise I've come down through the secret passage, and come after me,' thought Jack. 'I would be properly-caught then. But I don't see how they can think anything else. After all, all the doors were locked, and I didn't get out through the tower door or the scullery door – so they'll know I *must* have come this way. And if they remember that the tide is in, they will be able to come along and catch me beautifully.'

Jack really didn't know what to do. It was no use at all going back – and he certainly couldn't go forward unless he wanted to struggle with the tide in the cave.

'And I don't want to do that,' thought the boy, listening to the smack and gurgle of the big waves that swept into the large cave below. 'What in the world am

I to do?'

He suddenly thought that he could hear someone coming down the secret passage. He looked round the small cave in despair. Could he lock the door that led into the cave? No – the lock was broken many years ago.

He flashed his torch round the little cave. He suddenly saw a small hole in one corner. He bent down and shone his torch into it. It was a hole big enough for a small man to get through – but where did it lead?

There was no time to be lost. Jack wriggled through the hole somehow. It widened out a little in a moment or two and dipped down into the next cave. But as that was also full of swishing waves Jack could go no farther. The hole was simply a connection between the two caves, it seemed.

'Well, I simply can't do anything but wait here,' thought Jack. So he waited – and in a minute or two he heard the sound of people in the cave he had left, and heard voices.

'He's not here, Luiz,' said the voice of Mr Diaz. 'And he couldn't possibly have gone down through the shore cave, surely, or he would have been drowned.'

'Maybe he has tried, though,' said Luiz. 'He might have been very frightened, and have leapt into the water and tried to swim away.'

'Well, if so, he's gone,' said Mr Diaz. 'I can't imagine that *any* one could swim down there! Listen to the water sucking in and out. It would be impossible even for a man to swim through that.'

'Well, if he didn't go down there, where is he?' said Luiz rather sharply. 'You don't suggest that he is hiding in any of these small boxes, do you?'

'That's enough, Luiz,' said Mr Diaz, in an angry tone. 'I can't understand the whole thing – how did that boy get into the grounds and the house when the dogs were there? And how did he know about the secret passage? Where has he gone now? And what do you suppose he knows about the prince?'

'Well, if you really want to know what I think, I think that Anna the cook made a mistake,' said Luiz, sounding very bored. 'I think maybe something fell down in the scullery, and Anna rushed in – and *thought* she saw a boy! And she screamed and made a fuss.'

'Well, maybe you're right,' said Mr Diaz. 'Come on, let's go back. He's not here, anyway.'

Jack heard their scrambling footsteps going from the cave. For a while he caught the sound of their voices as they went up the secret passage. Then there was silence.

'My word, that *was* a narrow escape!' thought Jack. 'Good thing I found this hole. I wonder if the tide is going out? It sounds less strong.'

He wriggled himself into a different position, and was then able to switch on his torch and see the cave below. It was the one next to the large cave, and was only small. The sea was leaving it.

'It's safe to get down,' thought the boy, and he wriggled out of the small passage, slid down the cave wall and jumped down to the wet sand. A wave immediately ran into the cave and soaked Jack to the waist.

'You *would*!' said Jack to the wave. 'Just waiting for me, I suppose!'

The wave ran out. Jack ran quickly to the cave

entrance and looked up the beach. If he were quick, and dodged in between the big waves that ran up the sand and back, he could get up on the rocks, and climb along them to the cliff path.

Another wave ran up and Jack ran back into the cave to escape it. It swirled around his knees and nearly knocked him over. As soon as it ran out Jack ran out after it. He jumped quickly up on the rocks at the foot of the steep cliff. Another wave swept up and soaked his legs – but Jack clung to the rock and was safe.

He climbed a bit higher on to the rocks. Now the sea could hardly reach him, and as it was going down he would soon be safe.

He clambered over the rocks, stumbling and slipping on the seaweed. He came to the cliff path and put his feet on the steps cut out of the rock. He switched on his torch and went carefully up to the top of the cliff.

A wind was blowing there. Jack switched off his torch in case anyone saw its light, and made his way softly back to Peep-Hole. The gate creaked as he opened it. He was safe home at last!

He ran up the winding staircase and into his bedroom at the top. The others were there, and they crowded round him at once.

'Jack! Jack! What an age you've been! Were you nearly caught again?'

'You just listen to what happened to me tonight!' said Jack. 'I *have* had a time, I can tell you! My word, we had plenty of adventures on our secret island last year, but tonight's adventure was the most exciting of all!'

# A Plan to Rescue Paul

Jack told the others of his adventures that night. They listened in silence. When he came to the part about how he escaped down the secret passage to the shore, and could not get down into the cave because of the tide, Nora took hold of his hand tightly.

'You're not to go on adventures alone any more, Jack,' she said. 'Suppose you had been caught! We wouldn't have known *where* you were! Please, please, let us all go together in future, when there is anything to be done.'

'We'll see,' said Jack. 'Sometimes it's impossible for the whole lot of us to go together – we'd be noticed.'

'All the same, Nora's right,' said Mike. 'I think we ought to go out in pairs, Jack. You *have* had a time. What's going to be our next move?'

'Bed,' said Jack at once. 'I'm so sleepy. I can't keep my eyes open! We'll decide tomorrow what is to be done.'

The girls went down to their bedroom. Jack and Mike tumbled into their beds, and were soon asleep. Once again Dimmy had to wake them all, for they were *so* sleepy the next morning!

'You *have* turned into sleepyheads!' said Dimmy, in surprise. 'You will be very late for breakfast, so hurry up, please.'

The children put on their sunsuits, and raced downstairs. It was a beautiful sunny day, and they meant to bathe as soon as they could.

'Not till two hours after breakfast, remember,' said Dimmy warningly. 'It is dangerous to bathe after a big meal. Jack, I can trust you not to let the others do anything foolish, can't I?'

'Jack's our captain, Dimmy,' said Nora. 'We always do what he says.'

They went down to the beach, taking with them a basket of ripe plums from the garden for their eleven o'clock lunch. They chose a rock far down the beach, that the tide was already lapping round, and sat on it.

'It's best to be in some place where we can't possibly be overheard,' said Jack, looking all round. 'Now that Mr Diaz thinks one of us knows the secret of the prisoner in the tower, and all about the secret passage too, we shall have to be extra careful. I think Nora's right when she says we must go about together. Mr Diaz and Luiz would be pleased if they could catch any of us and keep us prisoner too!'

'Let's talk about rescuing Prince Paul,' said Nora, who was longing to get the boy out of the tower. 'Couldn't we take the rope ladder along tonight, Jack? Now that you've made friends with the dogs, it would be easy.'

'Well, I don't know if the dogs would be friends with you too,' said Jack doubtfully. 'We could try. No – I know what we'll do. I'll take Mike along with me to help, and you two girls can stay behind. We'll signal a message to Prince Paul with our big black letters today, then he will be ready to look out for the ladder tonight.'

The girls were disappointed at the thought of being

left behind, but they made no fuss. It was no use all of them going if the dogs barked at them and warned Mr Diaz that they were about. Perhaps they would be all right with just Jack and Mike.

'I'll take some meat along with me too, tonight,' said Mike. 'You can go into the grounds first, Jack, and fuss the dogs a bit – and then you can bring them to where I am and try to make them understand I am a friend, too.'

So it was all decided. The rescue was to take place that night. What fun! The children were so thrilled that they could hardly talk of anything else as they ate their plums at eleven o'clock, and then dug an enormous castle on the beach to sit on when the tide came in. It came swirling up the sand and soon surrounded their great castle.

They went back to Peep-Hole early, about noon, because for one thing the sea was rough and there was very little beach to play on, and for another thing they wanted to signal to Prince Paul. They got out their big letters and went to the window.

Prince Paul was in his tower, looking out. When he saw them he waved in delight. At once Jack began to send a message, holding out first one letter and then another. He spelt out quite a long message. Prince Paul hung half out of his window and waved as each word came to an end, to show that he had read it.

'Tonight look out for the rope ladder,' Jack spelt out.

Prince Paul made three letters with his fingers, one after the other. 'YES,' he spelt out. They were difficult letters to make with his fingers, and Jack, who was looking at Paul through the field-glasses, would hardly have known what they were if Paul hadn't nodded his head all the time to show that he meant yes.

'Cheer up,' Jack spelt out next. Paul waved and nodded again, then suddenly disappeared into the room. Jack at once came away from his window and pulled the others from it too.

'Somebody's come into Paul's room,' he said. 'He went away from the window so quickly. Yes – there's dear Mr Diaz looking across to our tower. Oh no, Mr Diaz, you won't see *us*! We're much too sharp for you!'

The others laughed. The dinner-bell went at that minute and they all rushed downstairs, only to be sent up again because in their excitement they had quite forgotten to wash their hands and do their hair.

'Sorry, Dimmy,' they said, when they arrived down clean at last. 'We were doing something exciting and quite forgot to tidy ourselves.'

'And what was this exciting thing you were doing?' asked Dimmy, ladling great helpings of garden peas on to their plates.

'It's a secret,' said Jack. 'A great big exciting secret, Dimmy! Wouldn't you love to know it?'

'I would,' said Dimmy. 'One of these days you will have to tell me.'

The others laughed. They did not know that very soon they would *have* to tell Dimmy their great big exciting secret!

They went boating with George the rest of the day. They caught some fish, and Dimmy said she would cook them for their supper.

'You're a good sort, Dimmy,' said Mike, giving her

a hug. 'Have you any meat-bones to spare? We'd like some tonight.'

Dimmy stared in surprise. 'What is all this mystery about meat at night?' she asked. 'Are you keeping some stray dogs up in your bedroom or something?'

The children squealed with laughter. 'No,' grinned Jack. 'It's all part of our secret, that's all, Dimmy.'

'Well, I won't ask any questions,' said Dimmy. 'If you want secrets, you can have them. There's an old mutton-bone you may have. Get it when you want it. It's in the larder.'

So Mike got the mutton-bone before he went to bed and put it into a bag. Jack was to carry the rope ladder. 'I think we'd better get to bed and try and have a sleep first,' said Jack, yawning. 'I feel very sleepy after my night out last night, Mike. We can set our alarm clocks for whatever time we like.'

'Well, I'll set it for half-past twelve,' said Mike. 'The moon will be up then, and we can see where we're going and what we're doing.'

So the alarm was set for half-past twelve and the four children settled into bed and went to sleep. The bell of the alarm clock rang loudly at half-past twelve and the two boys awoke. The girls heard it in their bedroom below, and slipped on their dressing-gowns ready to see the boys off.

Down the staircase went the children, Jack carrying the rope ladder and Mike carrying the mutton-bone. The girls whispered a goodbye and went back upstairs.

'Let's sit at the window of the boys' room,' said Nora. 'The moon is very bright now, and if we use the field-

glasses we can easily see what happens. It would be fun to see Prince Paul climbing down the rope ladder we made!'

So Nora and Peggy pulled a blanket over themselves and sat at the window of the boys' bedroom, keeping a watch on the window of the tower up the cliff. They took it in turns to use the field-glasses. How they wondered what the boys were doing!

Mike and Jack went silently up the cliff to the Old House. When they got there Jack whispered to Mike to stay outside the back gate whilst he went in to see if the dogs remembered him.

He slipped in softly. Tinker and Don were roaming about loose as usual. They smelt him and Don growled softly. Tinker came running up and licked his hand.

'Good dog, good dog,' said Jack in a low tone. He patted Tinker and then went softly to Don. Don sniffed round him, remembering the ham sandwiches and the biscuits that this boy had brought with him last time.

Jack took hold of the dogs' collars and led them to the back gate outside which Mike was waiting. The dogs growled when they saw Mike, but they did not bark. Mike held out the bone to them.

They were very hungry and they took the bone at once. They let Mike pat them. This boy seemed to be a friend of Jack's so they were not going to bark at him. They lay on the ground, growling and worrying at the big bone.

'Come on,' whispered Jack. Mike went with him to the bottom of the tower. A faint light shone at the top. Mike picked up a smooth round stone and took aim at the tower to warn Prince Paul they were there. The windows of the tower were open. Mike hoped to goodness he wouldn't smash the glass and waken everyone! However, he was good at throwing, so the stone went through the open window and landed neatly inside.

At once Prince Paul appeared at the window. 'Hello,' he said, in a low voice. 'I'm ready.'

Jack got hold of the stone to which the piece of string was firmly tied. It had a hole through the middle and the string was knotted through it. Jack took aim at the window.

The stone flew up in the air, carrying the length of thin string with it. It missed the window and fell down again. Jack picked it up. Once more he aimed – and this time the stone went right through the open window, just missing Paul, and landed on the floor.

Paul picked up the stone. He pulled at the string and it came up to the window pulling the strong twine behind it. Then Paul pulled at the twine, and the rope ladder began to unravel itself from Jack's hands and slip silently up the wall of the tower.

'There goes the ladder!' whispered Jack in excitement. 'Paul's got it! He's only got to fix it firmly to something and escape down it!'

Mike pulled on it gently. It felt tight to his hand. 'Paul's fixed it!' he whispered. 'It feels quite firm. I hope he gets a move on and comes down at once!'

But Paul didn't come! The boys waited and waited, but nobody came down the rope ladder. Whatever could have happened?

# Mike Is Caught

'Why doesn't Paul come?' wondered Jack impatiently. 'What a time he is! Surely the ladder is safe now.'

Mike peered up. The moon shone brightly on the tower of the Old House, and the rope ladder hung against the wall, quite straight and firm.

'It's funny,' said Mike. 'Do you suppose he doesn't dare to risk himself down our ladder?'

'Can't imagine *what* he's doing,' said Jack. 'We can't stand here all night. I do wish he'd hurry.'

The two dogs came running up. They had finished their bone. They nosed round the two boys, licking their hands. Jack patted them. 'Don't you bark at Paul when he comes down the ladder,' he warned them. 'He's a friend of ours – so don't you dare to make a sound. Do you hear, Tinker? Do you hear, Don?'

The dogs wagged their tails. They did not understand what Jack was saying, but they liked to hear him talking to them. Jack looked impatiently up the ladder once more. He shook it – but still nothing happened.

'I'll climb up softly and see what's up,' said Mike at last. 'He may be waiting for one of us to tell him how to climb down.'

'All right,' said Jack. 'I'll hold the ladder as firmly as I can. Good luck!'

Mike began to climb the rope ladder. He went up the side of the tower in the bright moonlight like a little black shadow. The girls at Peep-Hole could see him quite well through the field-glasses. They were puzzled to think why Mike should go up the ladder instead of Prince Paul coming down.

Mike went up and up. At last he came to the window where Prince Paul had taken in the top of the ladder. He put his head cautiously above the windowsill – caught sight of a little boy sitting on a couch at the far side of the room, looking very scared – and then a voice said, 'Got him!' and Mr Diaz leaned out of the window and

took firm hold of poor Mike!

Mike did not dare to struggle, for he was afraid of falling down the ladder. He had to let himself be hauled into the tower room. Mr Diaz stood him on the floor and then quickly pulled up the rope ladder, jerking it roughly from Jack's hands below.

'And now we have two prisoners,' said the soft sleepy voice of Luiz, and Mike saw that he was there too, standing behind Mr Diaz.

Mike said nothing. He just stood there, looking angry. He glanced at Prince Paul. The little boy called out to Mike.

'I would have warned you, but I dared not. They came into the room and saw me fixing the ladder – and they made me sit over here whilst they waited to see if you would come up.'

'And he came up,' said Mr Diaz. 'And here he can stay. And tomorrow, Luiz, we will board up this window so that neither Paul nor this inquisitive boy can signal to the other tiresome children. They must do without his company until Friday, when we take Paul somewhere that is not crowded out with curious children, who get themselves into trouble through poking their noses into somebody else's business.'

'You will have to miss a little of your holiday,' said sleepy-eyed Luiz to Mike. 'But Paul here will welcome your company, I am sure! Maybe this will teach you not to interfere another time in what is no business of yours!'

The two men went out of the tower-room, locked the door and bolted it, Mike shot to the window and leaned out.

'Jack! Jack!' he called in a low voice. 'Are you there?'

'Yes,' said Jack from behind a bush. 'What's happened?'

'They've pulled up the ladder and made me a prisoner too,' said Mike. 'But they don't know you're outside, Jack. Go back to the others and tell them and see if you can think of some idea to get us out. You won't be able to signal tomorrow because this window is going to be boarded up. You'll have to be jolly clever to rescue us. They are taking Paul away somewhere else on Friday and I expect they'll set me free then; but we *must* be rescued before or we'll never know where Paul has gone.'

Jack listened to this long whisper in silence. He was angry with himself for having let Mike go up the ladder. He might have thought that maybe someone was waiting up there to catch one of them. 'All right, Mike, old chap,' he said. 'I'll get you both out somehow. Cheer up. I'm going back now.'

He slipped through the bushes to the wall. He climbed up a tree, whilst the dogs whined below, sad to see him go, and then dropped on to the top of the high wall. He jumped from there to the ground, took a quick look round to see if anyone was about and then tore off in the moonlight to Peep-Hole.

The girls were waiting for him, both in tears, for they had seen all that had happened through their field-glasses.

'Oh, Jack, oh, Jack!' wept Nora. 'How can we get poor Mike back? Oh, why did you let him go up? We could see somebody waiting at the side of the window, and we couldn't warn you.'

'It was bad luck,' said Jack gloomily. 'I was an idiot to let him go up. Somehow I never thought of anyone lying in wait for one of us up there.'

'What are we going to do now?' asked Peggy, wiping her eyes. 'We'll have to get Mike back somehow. What will Dimmy say tomorrow morning when he doesn't go down to breakfast?'

'Cheer up,' he said. 'After all, we do know where Mike is – and we've only got to go to the police and they'll get him back for us.'

'There's only one fat old policeman here and he doesn't belong to Spiggy Holes,' said Peggy. 'And anyway we can't get him in the middle of the night.'

'I want to tell Dimmy,' said Nora suddenly. 'We will have to tell her tomorrow morning anyhow – and I want to tell her tonight. I can't go to sleep unless we tell somebody grown-up about Mike being caught.'

'But we can't wake Dimmy in the middle of the night!' said Jack. 'We'd better wait till the morning. Mike will be all right tonight; there's a bed in that tower-room, I saw it through the key-hole last night.'

'I want to tell Dimmy,' wept poor Nora. 'I do want to tell Dimmy.'

The little girl felt that if only she could tell somebody grownup something could be done. Grown-up people were powerful – she even had an idea that Dimmy might march up to the Old House straightaway and demand that Mike should be set free!

'Well, we'll go and wake Dimmy and tell her now, if you feel you must let her know tonight,' said Jack, who secretly felt as if he would like to tell her as soon as possible too. 'She may have a good idea.'

So down the winding staircase of their little tower went the three children, through the tower door into the kitchen and then up the carpeted staircase to Dimmy's bedroom. They knocked on the door.

'Who's that?' said Dimmy's voice.

'It's us,' said Nora. 'Can we come in?'

'Of course,' said Dimmy. 'Is one of you ill?'

The children opened the door. Dimmy switched on the light and sat up in bed and looked at them. Her hair was in two long plaits over her shoulder, and she somehow looked different, but very kind and anxious.

'Where's Mike?' she said. 'Is he ill?'

They sat on her bed, and first one and then another of the children told her the strange story of the Old House, the secret passage from the shore to the cellars of the Old House, the prince who was a prisoner in the tower – and then how Mike had been caught at the top of the rope ladder.

Dimmy listened in the greatest surprise and astonishment. She asked them questions, she exclaimed in amazement, she groaned with horror when she heard about Mike.

'Well!' she said, when the long story was finished, 'so that was your great secret! And a most extraordinary one too. I have wondered what those people up at the Old House were up to – I knew it was something strange and not quite right. Poor little Prince! What a shame to keep him prisoner like that! I read in the paper how he had disappeared, and no one knew where he was – but little did I think he was so near!'

'How are we to get Mike back?' asked Nora, much happier now that Dimmy knew everything. 'And Paul too – he must be rescued before Friday.'

Dimmy thought for a long time. Then she said something that set the children's hearts beating with excitement.

'My grandfather once told me that there was a secret way between Peep-Hole tower and the tower of the Old House,' she said. 'It was often used by the old-time smugglers when they wanted to get unseen from one house to the other. If we could find it, we could reach the towers of the Old House easily, and fetch back the two boys without anyone knowing.'

'Oh, Dimmy!' cried the three children, their eyes shining brightly. 'We *must* find it! We must, we must!'

'Well, we will hunt for it tomorrow,' said Dimmy. 'And I think we must get George to help us, because it will mean using a good deal of strength to find a passage that has been unused and hidden for years. As far as I remember, my grandfather said that a great stone had to be swivelled round in the wall of our tower – and certainly none of us could do that. George is very strong, and he can keep a secret too.'

After talking for a little while longer the children were sent off to bed. Before they got into bed they were very much cheered by seeing Mike at the lighted window of the Old House tower, waving to them in the moonlight. He seemed quite cheerful, and Nora and Peggy were very glad to see him.

'Good old Mike,' said Jack, getting into bed. 'I hope

he won't be too miserable.'

'So do I,' said Nora. 'And, oh, I do hope we find the hidden way between our tower and the other tower. Won't George be surprised when he hears all we've got to tell him! Oh, tomorrow, do come quickly!'

# Where Is the Secret Door?

The next morning when Jack rushed to the window to look at the tower of the Old House he found that Mr Diaz had kept his word – the window was now boarded up! No messages could be given to the prisoners, and they could send no messages back.

Jack didn't like it. He had hoped that perhaps Mr Diaz might have forgotten to block up the window. It made everything seem very serious, when he looked at that blind window with the boards across it.

The children went down to breakfast looking solemn. Nora gave a little sob when she looked at Mike's empty chair at the table. But Dimmy seemed very cheerful and patted her on the back.

'Don't worry,' she said. 'Now that you've told me, I'll do my best to help – and we'll rescue both boys, never fear!'

Nobody seemed to want much breakfast, although it was poached eggs, which they all loved. Nora was anxious to do something for Mike and Paul as soon as possible, and she wouldn't even let Dimmy wash up after breakfast.

'Please do let us see if we can discover the secret door out of our tower,' she begged. 'Leave the cups and things, Dimmy dear – we can do those afterwards.'

So Dimmy left them, and the three children trooped

up the winding stone staircase with her. They went to Jack's room and looked round the grey stone walls.

It seemed impossible to find any secret door in those great walls. They knocked on them, they pressed on them, they stood on chairs and pushed against the higher part of the walls, but nothing moved, nothing swung round to show a hidden passage in the thick stone walls.

At eleven o'clock they stopped their hunting, quite tired out. Dimmy looked at Nora's pale face, and was sorry for her.

'I'm going to make some cocoa for us all, and get some ginger cake,' she said. 'We need a rest.'

She ran downstairs. Peggy went with her to help. Nora sat on Jack's bed and looked gloomy.

'Cheer up, Nora,' said Jack.

'I'm quite, quite sure there's no hidden door in this room,' said Nora, with a deep sigh.

'I feel as if there isn't too,' said Jack anxiously. 'Wouldn't it be dreadful if it were only a tale, and not true at all!'

'Don't, Jack,' said Nora. 'You make me feel worse.'

Jack sat and thought for a few minutes. 'I wonder if by any chance Dimmy has any old maps of Spiggy Holes in that big bookcase of hers downstairs,' he said. 'If she has, one of them might show where the hidden door is.'

Dimmy came into the room at that minute, carrying a big jug of milky cocoa. Peggy followed with a dish of brown gingerbread. Everyone felt quite cheered by the look of it.

'Dimmy, I suppose you've no old books about Spiggy Holes, or old maps, have you?' asked Jack, munching his gingerbread.

Dimmy looked surprised. 'Why didn't I think of that before?' she said. 'Of course! There are two or three old books about this place, belonging to my great – grandfather. I believe they are very valuable. They are locked up in the big bookcase downstairs.'

Jack almost choked over his cake in his delight. 'Let's get them!' he said, jumping up.

'Finish your cake and cocoa,' said Dimmy. 'Then we'll go downstairs and look for them.'

How the three children swallowed down their cocoa and gingerbread, in their eagerness to rush downstairs to find the old books! It wasn't more than a minute or two before they were all in Dimmy's rather dark little drawing – room, watching her whilst she unlocked the big old – fashioned bookcase there.

She moved aside some of the books on the top row, and behind them were some very old books, carefully covered in thick brown paper.

'There they are,' said Dimmy. 'This one is called *Spiggy Holes* – a record of smuggling days. And this one is called *Tales of Smugglers*, and Spiggy Holes is mentioned several times. This one is only an old cookery book – and this is a diary kept by my grandfather.'

The children pounced eagerly on the first two books. The girls turned over the pages of *Spiggy Holes*, and Jack looked hurriedly through *Tales of Smugglers*.

'Look! Look! Here's a map of the secret passage we know!' cried Peggy suddenly. All the others crowded round her and peeped at the book she was holding. She laid it flat on the table. She pointed to a page on which was drawn a small map, showing Peep-Hole and the Old House and the shore. From the shore cave to the Old House the secret passage was shown winding its way through the cliff underground to the cellars of the Old House.

'But there's no way shown from Peep-Hole to the Old House,' said Jack in disappointment.

He was right. There was no hidden path between the two houses on the map. Eagerly Nora turned the pages to see if another map was shown, but there was none.

The two books were a great disappointment. Peggy, who was a good reader, hurriedly read through both of them to see if she could perhaps find anything written about the way between the two towers – but not a word was said.

'It must have been just a tale,' said Nora in disappointment, closing the books.

'I feel sure it wasn't,' said Dimmy, puzzled. 'I remember so well how my grandfather told me about the secret. I wonder if he says anything about it in his old diary. He kept it when he was a boy, and it wasn't found until a year or two ago. The ink has faded, and it was so difficult to read that I didn't try more than a few pages. It was all about his days as a boy.'

'Dimmy, let me have it,' said Jack. 'I will go away by myself and try to make it all out. It will take me a little time, but I'll use my magnifying glass to help me to read your grandfather's tiny writing.'

Dimmy gave the little paper-covered diary to Jack. He slipped off upstairs with it. The two girls looked at Dimmy.

'What shall *we* do?' asked Nora. 'I don't feel like bathing or digging without Mike here.'

'Then you can just come and help me to wash up those breakfast things and make the beds and dust and get dinner ready!' said Dimmy briskly. 'It will do you good to think of something else for a while.'

'It won't,' said Peggy dismally. But Dimmy was right. Both girls felt much better about things when they set to work to wash up and to dust.

Dinner-time came. Peggy went up to fetch Jack. He was huddled in a corner with his magnifying glass, trying to read every word of the old, old diary.

'Dinner-time,' said Peggy. 'Have you found anything interesting, Jack?'

'No,' said Jack. 'It's all about how he goes birds'-nesting and fishing and boating. He must have been a nice sort of boy. He was a great one for playing tricks on people too. It says here how he put a toad into his aunt's bed, and she woke the whole house up to get it out!'

'Naughty boy!' said Peggy. 'And poor old toad! It must have hated being squashed under the bedclothes. What else does it say?'

'Oh, lots of things,' said Jack, flicking over the pages. 'Tell Dimmy I'll be down in half a minute. I just want to finish the next few pages.'

So Peggy went downstairs again, and Dimmy and the two girls began their meal without Jack. They were in the middle of it when they heard a tremendous shouting, and Jack's feet came tearing down the stone staircase. The door into the kitchen was flung open, and then the dining room door flew back with a crash. The girls almost jumped out of their skin. Dimmy leapt to her feet.

'Whatever's the matter?' she cried.

119

'I've found it, I've found it!' yelled Jack, dancing round the room like a clown in a circus. 'It's all here – there's a map of it and everything!'

The girls squealed. Dimmy sank down into her chair again. She wasn't used to these adventures!

'Show! Show us the map!' yelled Nora. She swept aside her plate and glass with a crash, and Jack set the old diary down on the tablecloth.

'Listen,' he said. 'This is Dimmy's grandfather's entry for the third of June, exactly one hundred years ago! He says, "Today has been the most exciting day of my life. I found at last the old hidden passage between Peep-Hole and the Old House tower. A gull fell into the chimney of my room and I climbed up it to free the bird. Whilst I was there I pressed by accident on the great stone that swings round to open the passage in the wall of the tower."'

'O-o-oh!' squealed Nora. 'We can find it too!'

'Don't interrupt,' said Peggy, her face pale with excitement. 'Go on, Jack.'

'He goes on to tell how he got into the passage, which runs down the walls of our tower to the ground, up the cliff to the Old House, branches off to join our own secret passage somewhere, and also goes on to the tower of the Old House, up and inside the thick walls there, and into the topmost room of the tower!' Jack could hardly speak, he was so thrilled at having found what he wanted.

'There's a rough map here that he drew after he had found out all about the passage. He kept the secret to himself, because he was afraid that if he didn't his father might have the passage blocked up.'

Everyone pored over the map. It was faded and difficult to see, even under the magnifying glass, but the children could plainly follow the passage from their tower, downwards in the wall right to the ground and below it, then underground to the Old House, up through the thick walls there, and into the top room of the Old House tower.

'I knew I was right! I knew I was right!' said Dimmy, quite as excited as the children.

'Let's go straight up and find it!' said Nora. 'Come on! Oh, do come on!'

They all fled upstairs, tumbling over the steps in their haste. They *must* find that secret door in the chimney. Quick! Quick!

# Another Secret Passage!

They all rushed into Jack's bedroom at the top of the tower – but at the first look round Peggy gave a cry.

'What sillies we are! There's no fireplace here!'

'Goodness – of course not,' said Jack in dismay. 'I'd completely forgotten that. But the map quite clearly shows that the passage starts somewhere in the chimney.'

'Our room below has a big stone fireplace!' cried Nora. 'It must be there that the passage starts. Hurry!'

Down they tore to Nora's room, where there was certainly a big, old-fashioned stone fireplace. Jack looked up it.

'Get me a stool or something,' he said. 'I can stand on that and grope about.'

So, with the girls jigging impatiently about below, Jack stood on a stool and groped about in the dirty old chimney. At one side he felt what seemed to him to be narrow steps cut in the chimney. He told Miss Dimmy, looking down at her as black as a little sweep!

'Yes, that's right, there would be steps there,' said Dimmy. 'In the olden days small boys were sent up to sweep these big chimneys and sometimes steps were cut to help them. Can you get up them, Jack?'

Jack thought he could. So up he went, choking over

the years-old soot. The steps were very small, and came unexpectedly to a little opening off the chimney itself. Jack was sure that the door to the hidden passage was somewhere in that opening!

The stones and bricks were intermixed there and were rough to his hand. He pulled and pushed at each one, hoping it would swing round and show him an opening beyond. But not until he suddenly slipped and bumped against a certain stone did anything move at all!

His shoulder fell against a stone that stood out from the rest. It gave under his weight, and seemed to swing round, giving a click as it did so. Jack quickly shone his torch on to it, and saw a small hole appearing in the wall of the chimney. He put his hand into the hole and felt an iron ring.

'I've found the entrance! I've found it!' he yelled down the chimney. He pulled hard at the iron ring, and felt the stone to which it was fastened move a little; but no matter how hard Jack pulled he could not make the stone move any farther.

He climbed down the chimney, and the girls cried out in horror when they saw his black face and hands. He grinned at them, and his teeth shone white in his mouth.

'Dimmy, we'll have to get George to help us,' he said. 'I think the entrance stone is stiff with the years that have gone by since it was last used. If we got George to bring a thick rope and fasten it to the iron ring I've found up there, we could swing the stone round all right and see the entrance to the passage. The stone has moved just a little – I can see the crack with my torch where it should come away from its place.'

'George is working in the garden this afternoon,' said Dimmy joyfully. 'We can get him easily. No, Jack, no, don't you go and get him – you look so awful!'

But Jack was gone. He sped down the staircase and out into the garden. George was busy digging up potatoes. Jack burst on him, crying, 'George, George, come quickly!'

George looked up in surprise, and saw a black, grinning creature running towards him. He got a tremendous shock and dropped his spade. It took him quite a minute before he would believe that the black creature was his friend Jack!

Talking eagerly and telling George things that astonished the farm lad greatly, Jack led him up the stone staircase to the girls' bedroom.

'Has he brought a rope?' cried Nora.

George nearly always had a rope tied two or three times round his waist. He gaped at the two girls and Miss Dimmy, and then said, 'Where's Mike?'

'You haven't been listening!' said Jack impatiently. 'I was telling you all the way up.'

'Let *me* tell him,' said Dimmy, seeing that George really was thinking that everyone was quite mad. So she told him the whole story as shortly as possible. George nodded his head solemnly every now and again. He didn't really seem astonished now that he knew everything, but his eyes gleamed when he heard that Dimmy wanted him to go up the chimney and tie his rope to the iron ring.

'I'd like to get Mike back all right,' said George, undoing the rope round his middle. It proved to be very long and very strong. He disappeared into the chimney with Jack's torch. Jack tried to climb up after him, he was so impatient, but came down at once, his eyes and mouth full of soot kicked down by George's enormous boots.

George found the iron ring in the little opening and knotted his rope in it. The end fell down the chimney to the hearth like a brown snake. George jumped down.

'Now we'll all pull,' he said, with his slow, wide smile. So they all pulled – and the rope gave a little as the big stone above swung round and back, leaving just enough room for anyone to squeeze through.

Jack climbed up the chimney again and gave a shout as he saw the dark opening. 'Oh, the secret passage is here all right! Come on, all of you!'

Poor Dimmy! She was really horrified at seeing everyone go up that dirty, dark old chimney and getting black with soot – but even she went up too, just to see what kind of a secret passage it could be!

George had squeezed through the opening that was made when one big stone had swung out of its place. It had been cunningly built on a kind of swivel set in the next stone, and when weight was put on to the iron ring the stone swung round.

A very narrow way led round the back of the chimney – so narrow that George had to walk sideways to make himself small enough. Then he came to an iron ladder set at his feet, disappearing down into the darkness. He called back to the children.

'There's a ladder here, going downwards. I reckon there's an outer wall and an inner wall to part of this tower, and that's where the passage is! The rest of the tower wall is solid.'

Down the narrow iron ladder they all went. They had to hold their torches in their teeth, for they needed both their hands. Dimmy had no torch, so she stood at the top of the ladder, waiting for them all to return.

The iron ladder went right down inside the wall and ended below the tower itself. A small room was at the foot of the ladder, and in it the children saw two old tops, a wooden hand-carved toy boat and some old, mildewed books.

'This must have been Dimmy's grandfather's hidey-hole when he was a boy,' said Jack. 'Look at his toys!'

From this small underground room, smelling so musty and damp, a narrow passage led up the cliff.

'This passage can't be so very far underground,' said George, leading the way. 'Hello! Look there! Surely that is daylight?'

It was! A bright circle of daylight shone not far above their heads.

'I guess a rabbit has made its burrow above us,' said Jack, with a laugh. 'He must have burrowed from the surface down to this passage. What a shock for him when he fell through!'

'Well, the bunny has let some fresh air into this place, at any rate,' said George. 'Perhaps that is what has kept it fresh enough to breathe in.'

They went along the passage, and then came to a stop. 'What's up, George? Why have you stopped!'

asked Jack.

'Because the passage has fallen in here,' said George. 'We'll have to get spades and dig it free again. The roof has fallen in, and we can't get any farther. We'll come back and dig it out. I reckon the passage goes on to the tower of the Old House, and then we'll find an iron ladder going up inside the walls just as we found at Peep-Hole.'

The children squeezed back through the passage and went up the iron ladder to the chimney. Dimmy had got down again and was waiting for them in the girls' room, having washed herself clean.

They told her excitedly what they had found. Jack ran down to the shed to get spades, and to find some biscuits for himself, for he had had no dinner.

'We shall be able to rescue Mike and Paul very soon now,' said Peggy hopefully.

'Better clear the passage now and try to get to the boys tonight,' said George thoughtfully. 'You see, if we can rescue them at night there's not so much fear of us being heard, and we can get a good few hours' start on the folk at the Old House.'

'Right, George,' said Dimmy, who was just as excited as the children.

George and Jack went to clear the passage ready for the night's adventure. The girls went to wash themselves, and to pore once more over the exciting diary that had told them just what they wanted to know.

In an hour's time Jack and George came back, hot, dusty, sooty, and thirsty. Dimmy made them have a bath, and put on clean clothes – though George looked very comical in Mike's shorts and jersey! Then they all sat down to a good tea, which they really felt they had earned.

'This is getting more and more exciting!' said Peggy, spreading her bread and butter with Dimmy's homemade shrimp paste. 'I feel as if I'm bursting with excitement. If only old Mike knew what we were doing!'

'He'll know soon enough,' said Jack, with his mouth full.

'I reckon the strange folk up at the Old House will be pretty furious when they find Mike and the prince gone,' said George rather solemnly. 'I think you'd better all get away from here with Paul, whilst Miss Dimity and I tell the police and find out a bit more about this prince of yours.'

'Get away from here?' said Jack. 'But where could we go that was safe?'

No sooner had he said it than he and the girls had the most marvellous idea in the world.

'Our secret island! We'd be safe there! It's not far from here!' yelled Jack.

'The secret island!' cried Peggy and Nora.

'What's that?' asked George in astonishment.

'It's on Lake Wildwater, about forty miles from here,' said Jack. 'We lived on our secret island on the lake when we ran away once – it would be a wonderful place for the prince till he's safe from his enemies.'

'Good idea!' said George. 'I'll take you round the coast in my boat to Longrigg, where I've a brother who has a car. He can drive you to Wildwater – and you can do the rest!'

'Won't Mike be pleased, won't Mike be pleased!' shouted Nora. 'Oh, I do feel so happy!' And she danced poor Dimmy round and round the room till Dimmy had to beg for mercy!

# The Rescue of the Prisoners

It was arranged that Mike and Paul should be rescued that night through the secret passage – if only the entrance at the other end could be used and was not too old or stiff!

'Jack and I went right along the passage to the Old House tower,' said George. 'There's an iron ladder there like ours. I reckon it leads up to the top room, to the fireplace.'

'We had better plan everything carefully,' said Dimmy. 'George and Jack had better rescue the boys, and bring them safely back here. Then I and the girls will prepare plenty of food and take it down to George's boat. We will wait there for you.'

'Yes, we shall need plenty of food on the secret island,' said Nora. 'There are wild raspberries there, and wild strawberries, but that's about all, unless we catch rabbits and fish as we did last year when we lived there!'

'You'll only be there a day or two until we can find out about Prince Paul and get someone to take charge of him till he goes back to his own land,' said Dimmy. 'I will stay behind here – and George will return to me, too, so that I shall be able to deal with the folk at the Old House. I shall simply say that you have all gone away.'

'Dimmy, let's get the food ready for tonight,' said

Peggy eagerly. 'We only need food – we don't need saucepans or kettles, or beds or anything like that – everything is neatly stored away in the dry caves on the secret island, ready for when we went there again. But we shall need plenty of food for five people.'

So the two girls and Dimmy began to pack up all kinds of food. There was a joint of meat, two dozen tarts, a tin of cakes of all kinds, a tin of biscuits, some tins of soup and fruit, potatoes and peas from the garden, and a basket of ripe plums. Cocoa was put into the box of food, and tins of milk. Nora remembered the sugar, and Peggy thought of the salt. It was really exciting packing everything up.

George carried the big box down to the boat and stowed it there. Jack followed with two baskets. Dimmy hurriedly stuffed a box of blackcurrant lozenges into one basket, in case any of them caught cold that night.

'I think that's everything,' said Dimmy. 'You must wear your coats tonight, for the weather is a bit colder. Good gracious me, what an adventure this is! I never thought I'd have such a time at my age!'

'Dimmy dear, I wish you were coming with us to our lovely secret island,' said Peggy. 'You'd love it so. You'll be lonely without us here, won't you?'

'Yes,' said Dimmy. 'But perhaps you'll soon be back again. Anyway, it will be nice to have Mike safe. I don't like to think of him up there in that tower all the time.'

The night came quickly, for they had all been busy. It was arranged that George and Jack should go to rescue the two boys about half-past eleven. George had already been to the next village and had rung up his brother at

Longrigg to tell him to have a car ready for the children. In fact, George was really marvellous.

'Now it's time to go,' said George, looking at the enormous watch he kept in his waistcoat pocket. 'Miss Dimity, you will go down to my boat with the girls, won't you, in a few minutes. Jack and I will bring the boys back here by the secret passage and slip down to the boat too. Then we can set off.'

'Good luck, George!' said Nora. 'Good luck, Jack!'

Dimmy and the girls went to the tower room with them and watched them climb up the chimney. They heard them groping round the narrow way behind the chimney to the iron ladder. Then there was silence.

'We'd better get Mike's coat and an extra coat for Prince Paul,' said Dimmy. 'Then we'll make our way to the beach and sit in the boat till the others come. I'll just give you both a drink of hot milk first, for I can see you are shivering!'

'It's with excitement, not with cold,' said Nora. But she was glad of the hot milk all the same.

'I do wonder how George and Jack are getting on,' said Peggy. 'I wonder if they've reached the Old House tower yet.'

George and Jack were getting on very well. They had climbed down the iron ladder, their torches between their teeth. They had gone through the little room below, where the old, old toys still lay, and had made their way through the narrow passage underground that led to the Old House.

When they came to the part where they had cleared away the fallen roof that afternoon George shone his torch round. 'It looks to me as if another bit of the roof will fall in at any moment,' said George anxiously. 'I hope it lasts till we get back.'

'So do I,' said Jack. 'It would be awful to be caught because the roof fell in. Gracious, George – a bit of it's tumbling in now – some stones fell on my coat.'

'Well, let's hope for the best,' said George. 'Come on.'

On they went, and presently came to where another narrow passage forked off from the one they were following.

'That's the passage to the secret way between the shore cave and the cellars of the Old House,' said Jack. 'It's a pity that is blocked up too, George, or we might have tried it.'

The two had already seen that afternoon that the passage joining theirs to the shore cave passage was blocked up with fallen stones, and they had not tried to clear it, for, as George said, it might be blocked up all the way. It was quicker to use the passage from one tower to the other, and to return to Peep-Hole and run down to the beach by the cliff path.

They soon came to the iron ladder that led up the inside of the walls of the Old House tower. They climbed it as quietly as they could. They came to a narrow ledge running round the back of a chimney place. They squeezed round it, and found themselves in a small dark place with stone walls all around.

'Feel for an iron ring,' whispered George. 'There is sure to be one here. If we can find it, we'll slip my rope into it, and both pull hard. I reckon the stone will swivel round just like ours at Peep-Hole did.'

So they felt about for an iron ring, and shone their torches here and there – and at last George found the ring! He slipped his rope into it and knotted it. Then he and Jack pulled this way and that way – and suddenly the stone in which the iron ring was set groaned a little, swung slowly round – and there, in front of George and Jack, was the entrance to the fireplace built in the top room of the Old House tower!

Voices came up from the room below. George and Jack stood perfectly still and listened. Mr Diaz was speaking.

'At dawn tomorrow you will come with me, Paul – and we will leave Mike here for a few days, just to give him a lesson not to put his nose into things that don't concern him! Anna will see to him, and set him free next week.'

'Where are you taking Paul?' asked Mike's voice.

'Wouldn't you like to know?' said Mr Diaz in a mocking voice.

'Yes, I would,' said Mike. 'You've no right to make any boy a prisoner, Mr Diaz, and you'll get punished soon.'

'Be careful I don't punish you first, you impudent boy!' said Mr Diaz angrily. 'Now go to bed, both of you – but you, Paul, must not get undressed, for you must be ready to come with me when I fetch you at dawn.'

There was the sound of a door closing. George and Jack heard a key being turned and bolts being shot into their place. Then they heard footsteps going down the winding stone staircase.

'Wait a few minutes in case he comes back,' whispered George, as he felt Jack move forward. They waited.

They heard Mike comforting poor Paul. Jack felt furiously angry with Mr Diaz. If only he could have him well punished!

'Now,' whispered George. The two squeezed themselves through the narrow opening into the chimney. Below were rough steps. They felt for them with their feet.

Mike and Paul heard the noise and looked at one another in surprise.

'What's that noise, Mike?' asked Paul.

'A bird in the chimney perhaps,' said Mike.

'Yes!' came Jack's voice. 'It's a jack-daw, Mike! It's Jack!'

Paul got such a shock that he sat down suddenly on a chair that wasn't there. Mike got a shock too, but a very unpleasant one. He ran to the chimney and peered up – only to get a mass of soot in his face!

'Jack! Jack! How in the world did you get there?' asked Mike, in the greatest amazement and surprise. 'Are the girls with you?'

'No. Only George,' said Jack, jumping lightly down and stooping to get out of the hearth. 'Come on, George.'

Prince Paul picked himself up and stared in surprise at the two black-faced people coming from the chimney. Then he solemnly bowed to them and shook hands.

'We'll tell all there is to tell later on,' said George. 'There's no time to lose now. Dawn comes in a few hours and Mr Diaz will be back to take Paul with him, so we have only that time to get you away safely. Come along back with us now – this hidden way that we have found leads back to Peep-Hole.'

'The girls and Dimmy are waiting with lots of food in George's boat,' Jack said excitedly to Mike. 'We're going to the secret island, Mike. Think of it!'

Paul knew all about the secret island, for Mike had told him about it whilst the two had been prisoners together. His pale little face lighted up with joy. He took Mike's arm and squeezed it.

'Let's go quickly,' he begged. So George took Paul, and Mike followed Jack, and they all disappeared up the chimney, leaving behind on the floor a great mass of soot.

Down the iron ladder they climbed, Paul a bit afraid for he was not used to adventures of this sort. Then along the hidden way they went in single file.

But suddenly George, who was leading, stopped in dismay. The others bumped into him.

'What's up, George?' asked Jack.

'Just what I feared!' groaned George. 'The roof's fallen in again – and it's a bad fall this time. We'll never clear it! We're trapped!'

Jack pressed by George and looked at the fall of earth and stones in silence. It was true. It was a very bad fall – *now* what were they to do?

# An Exciting Time

'Goodness, George! Whatever shall we do now?' said Jack anxiously. 'We can never clear that fall – it looks as if the roof has fallen in for yards! We can't go back to the Old House – we'd just be walking into danger!'

George rubbed his chin and thought hard. They couldn't go forward – they couldn't go back – and certainly they couldn't stay in the middle!

'Seems as if we'd better go and have a look at that other blocked-up passage,' said George at last. 'You know – the one that branches off this one to join the secret way between the shore cave and the cellars of the Old House.'

'Right,' said Jack. 'The block there may not be so bad as it looks. It's our only chance anyway.'

They all went to the place where the passage branched off. They squeezed down it till they came to the block. George pulled away some of the stones and tried to see how much of the passage was stopped up.

'I believe if the four of us could work at it we might clear it in time,' said George at last. 'And I've got a good idea too – the block is mostly of stones and bits of rock. If I pick them up, pass them to Jack, and he passes them to Paul and Paul to Mike, Mike could pile them up behind him and make them look as if there has been a

good old roof-fall there! So if Mr Diaz does come along he'll think it's impossible to come this way. And we'll be safely on the other side of the stones!'

'Good old George!' said Mike and Jack, who always loved a good idea. 'Come on – we'll start.'

'What do I do?' asked Paul, who was half-frightened, half-thrilled at being with the others. They told him what to do.

'You only just take hold of the stones I pass you,' said Jack, 'and make them behind to Mike.'

They set to work. George cleared away the stones, passing them to the others. Mike threw them behind him, and soon a great pile lay there, looking exactly as if they had fallen from the roof of the passage!

Soon George had cleared away quite a bit of the block. He shone his torch up and down it, and gave a cry of joy.

'I believe it'll be all right, boys! I can see the passage beyond already. We'll only need to clear a bit more, and we shall have a hole big enough to squeeze through.'

They worked and worked. Paul became tired and they had to let him have a rest. Two hours went by. George felt rather anxious. He did not want Mr Diaz to discover that Paul and Mike had escaped before they had all got safely away in the boat.

At last there was a hole big enough to squeeze through. One by one they got through it, and then George did a funny thing.

He glanced up at the roof near the block and then, taking a big stone, he struck the roof hard. A shower of earth fell at once.

'George! What are you doing?' cried Jack.

'I'm just making a small roof-fall,' grinned George, his teeth flashing in the light of Jack's torch. 'If I can fill up the hole we've made in the block, we'll be all right. We don't want our dear friend Mr Diaz to squeeze

141

through the hole too!'

'Good idea,' said Jack. 'Now hadn't we better go on, George? It's getting late.'

'Sh!' said George suddenly. Everyone stood perfectly quiet in the passage. 'Switch off your torches,' whispered George. 'I can hear something.'

They all switched off their torches. Sounds were coming near – voices – angry voices!

'Oh, do let's go,' whispered Mike. But George shook his head in the darkness and whispered. 'No.'

'We don't want them to hear us,' he said in a low tone. 'They may guess where this leads to if they hear us, and go rushing off to the beach to find our boat. I think we're safe enough if we keep quiet. Put your arm round Paul, Jack – he's frightened, poor kid!'

They stood there in perfect silence. They heard Mr Diaz and Luiz and someone else talking. They came to the roof-fall in the other passage and exclaimed about it.

'Look at that! They can't have gone down that way!'

'It might have fallen *after* they had gone,' said the sleepy voice of Luiz. Then a sharper voice spoke loudly.

'This is disgraceful – to let the boy slip through your fingers like this! Are you sure there is no other way out of this passage?'

'There's a branch off it somewhere here,' came Luiz's voice. Footsteps came up to the blockage through which George and the others had managed to squeeze.

'There's a great pile of stones here,' said Mr Diaz, peering over the stones that the boys had piled up. 'And another roof-fall or something beyond. They couldn't possibly have got through that. No, it looks as if they escaped down that passage to Peep-Hole, and the roof fell after they had gone through. Well, our best course is to go back to the Old House and make a raid on Peep-Hole. The boys are sure to be there.'

The voices and the footsteps grew fainter. At last they could no longer be heard. Everybody sighed with relief.

'Now we can get on,' said George cheerfully. 'I thought somehow they wouldn't guess we'd gone this way – and anyway they don't know that it leads down to the passage to the shore cave. Come on!'

They stumbled down the secret passage and at last came to an opening in the ground at their feet. Jack shone his torch down.

'This is where our passage joins the shore-passage,' he cried in excitement. 'We'll have to jump down into it. No wonder we didn't spot it when we used the shore-passage – we didn't dream of looking for holes in the roof, did we?'

They all jumped down into the passage below. Then they made their way quickly to the cave, sliding down into it, holding safely to the rope that swung there to help them.

'I wonder if the girls are there in the boat all right,' said Mike.

The girls *were* there! They had been there for hours, anxiously waiting with Dimmy. They had not been able to imagine what could have happened to everyone!

They had talked at first, and then had watched and waited for the boys. But they hadn't come. Then Nora had begun to worry.

'Oh dear! They ought to be here now. Whatever can have happened?'

'Perhaps Mr Diaz or someone was in the room for ages with Mike and Paul,' said Peggy sensibly. 'Jack and George couldn't possibly rescue them if anyone was with the others.'

'That's true,' said Dimmy. 'Well, we must wait in patience. We can't do anything else! Are you two warm enough?'

'I'm glad of my coat,' said Peggy. 'It's a funny thing, but excitement makes me feel rather cold!'

They waited for another hour. Now all of them were anxious and worried, though Dimmy tried not to show it. Then Nora gave a low cry.

'Look! I can see the light of a torch over there in the shore cave! It must be them!'

It was! Jack, Mike, Paul, and George hurried across the sand in silence. They were tired and stiff now, but they knew that a long row awaited them! They were pleased that everything had at last gone well.

'Oh, Mike, dear Mike!' said Nora joyfully, so glad to have her brother back again that the tears fell down her cold cheeks. Mike hugged her and Peggy kissed kind old Dimmy, and got into the boat with the others. It was a good thing it was a big boat!

'I must say goodbye,' said Dimmy hurriedly. 'Don't push off yet, George – you've forgotten I'm not going with you!'

'Oh, Dimmy, I *wish* you were coming too,' said Peggy, sad to say goodbye to her. 'I hope you'll be all right. Anyway, George will be with you as soon as he rows the boat back from Longrigg.'

'Goodbye, dears,' whispered Dimmy. She got out of the boat. 'Take care of yourselves. I'll let you know as soon as we have found out about Prince Paul, and what we must do with him. Good luck!'

'Good luck!' whispered the children. George pushed off from the little wooden jetty. The boat floated out on the water. George bent to the oars and began to row away. Soon nothing could be seen of Dimmy at all – she had vanished into the darkness.

The boat went on and on over the dark, restless sea. Jack had found the second pair of oars and was rowing too, to help George. The children spoke to one another in whispers, because George said voices carried so far over the water.

'Well, we've rescued you, Paul!' said Jack. 'You're safe with us now! And I don't somehow think that Mr Diaz will be able to find you on our secret island! We'll have a nice little holiday there for a few days – and oh, won't it be *lovely* to be back there again, all by ourselves!'

'Lovely, lovely, lovely!' said the others, and began to dream about their island. Soon, soon, they would be there!

# Off to the Secret Island

George rowed the boat silently over the calm sea towards the little fishing village of Longrigg. Jack helped him, and the children sat quietly in the boat until George said it was safe to talk.

'No one can hear you now,' he said. 'So talk away!'

And then what a noise there was as Mike told the others all that had happened when he was a prisoner with Paul. And Paul joined in excitedly, telling how he had been captured in his own father's palace and taken away to Cornwall over sea and land, in ships, aeroplanes, and cars. Poor Paul! He was really very glad to be with friends once more, for although he had not been very badly treated by Mr Diaz and Luiz, he had been kept a close prisoner for some time.

Soon the moon came up and flooded the sea with its silvery light. The children could see one another's faces as they talked, and every time the oars were lifted from the water silvery drops fell off the blades.

'There's Longrigg!' said George, as they went round a cliff that jutted out into the sea. Everybody looked. The children had been to Longrigg before with George in his boat, but it looked different now in the moonlight – a huddle of silvery houses set in a cove between the cliffs.

'It's like an enchanted village,' said Nora dreamily.

'And I guess our secret island will look enchanted too, tonight, when we get there. Oh, I do feel so very excited when I think that we're really going there again!'

The children began to talk of their adventure on the secret island the year before – how they had kept their own cow there and their own hens. How they had built their own house of willows, and had found caves in the hillside to live in during the winter. Paul listened, and longed to see the wonderful island!

They landed at Longrigg. George took them through the deserted village street to his brother's garage, a tiny place at the top of the street. A man was there waiting for them.

'Hello, Jim,' said George. 'Here are the passengers for your trip. And mind, Jim, not a word to anyone about this. I'll explain everything to you when you come to see me tomorrow. Till then, say nothing to anybody.'

'Right, George,' said Jim, who seemed very like his brother as he stood there, sturdy and straight in his dark overalls.

'Goodbye, George, and thanks for all your help,' said Jack, getting into the car with the others. 'Have we got the food? Oh yes – it's in the back. Good!'

'Goodbye,' said George. 'I'm going back to Peep-Hole now in case Miss Dimity wants a bit of help. Stay on your secret island till you hear from us. You'll all be quite safe there!'

The car started up and Jim set off up the cliff road. The children waved to George, and then the car turned a bend and was out of sight. They were on their way to Lake Wildwater – on their way to the island!

It was about forty miles away, and the car purred softly through the moonlit night. Paul was very sleepy and went sound asleep beside Peggy – but the others were too excited to sleep.

Jack watched the country flash by – five miles gone, ten, twenty, thirty, forty! They were almost there. Jim was to drive to where the children's aunt and uncle had once lived, and then leave them. They could find their way then to the lake, and get their boat, which was always ready.

'Here we are,' said Jim. The car stopped. Jim got out. 'I'll give you a hand with the food down to the boat,' he said. So the six of them carried the food to where the boat was locked up in a small boathouse. Captain Arnold, the children's father, had built them a little house for their boat in case they wished to visit their secret island at any time. Mike had the key on his key ring. He got it out and unlocked the boathouse. There lay the boat, dreaming of the water. The moon shone into the boathouse, and Jack was able to see quite well, as he undid the rope and pushed the boat from the house.

The food was put in. Everyone but Jim got into the boat. Jim said goodbye and good luck and strode back over the fields to his waiting car. The five children were alone!

Jack and Mike took the oars. Paul was wide awake now and was full of excitement, longing to see this wonderful secret island that he had heard so much about.

'It won't be long now,' said Nora, her eyes shining happily in the moonlight. The oars made a pleasant splashing sound in the silvery waters, and the boat glided along smoothly.

On and on they went – and then, rounding a corner of the wooded bank of the lake, they came suddenly in sight of their island!

'Look! There it is, Paul!' cried Peggy. Paul looked. He saw a small island floating on the moonlit lake, with trees growing down to the water's edge. It had a hill in the middle of it, and it looked a most beautiful and enchanting place.

'Our secret island,' said Nora softly, her eyes full of happy tears, for she had loved their island with all her heart, and had spent many, many happy days there along with the others the year before.

For a while the two boys leaned on their oars and looked silently at their island, remembering their adventures there. Then they rowed quickly again, longing to land on the little beach they knew so well.

'There's our beach, with its silvery sand all glittering in the moonlight!' cried Nora. The boat slid towards it and grounded softly in the sand. Jack leapt out and pulled the boat in. One by one the children got out and stood on the little sloping beach.

'Welcome to our island, Paul,' said Peggy, putting her arm round the excited boy. 'This is our very own. Our father bought it for us after our adventures here last year – but we didn't think we'd visit it this summer! We left it last Christmas, when we were living in the hill caves. They were so cosy!'

'Come along up the hill and find the caves,' said Jack. 'We are all awfully tired, and we ought to get some sleep. We'll get the rugs and things out of the cave, and

heat some cocoa and have a meal. Then I vote we make our beds on the heather, as we used to do. It's very hot tonight, and we shall be quite warm enough.'

'Hurrah!' said Mike in delight. 'Give me a hand with this box of food. The girls can bring the other things, if Paul will help them.'

'Of course I will,' said Paul, who really felt as if he was living in a peculiar dream! They all made their way up the beach, through a thicket of bushes and trees, and up a hillside where the bracken was almost as tall as they were. The moon still shone down from a perfectly clear sky, and except that the colours were not there, everything was as clear as in daylight.

'Here's our cave!' said Jack in delight. 'The heather and bracken are so thick in front of it that I could hardly see it. Mike, have you got your torch handy? We shall need to go into our inner store cave to get a few things tonight.'

Mike fished in his pocket for his torch. He gave it to Jack. 'Thanks,' said Jack. 'Peggy, come with me into the store cave, will you, and we'll get out the rugs. Mike, will you and Nora choose a place for a fire and make one? We'll have to have some cocoa or something. I'm so hungry and thirsty that I could eat grass!'

'Right, Captain!' said Nora, feeling very happy indeed. It was wonderful to be on the island like this – able to sleep in the heather and have a campfire. She and Mike and Paul hunted about for twigs and wood, and found a nice open place near the cave for the fire.

Peggy and Jack went to the back of the cave, found the passage that led into the inner cave, and crept through to the big store cave beyond that lay in the heart of the hillside

'Everything's here just as we left it!' said Peggy, pleased, as Jack shone his torch around. 'Oh, there's the kettle, Jack – and I want a saucepan, too, for the soup tonight and eggs tomorrow morning. Dimmy put some into the box. Look, there's the rabbit-skin rug we made last year – and the old blankets and rugs too. Bring those, Jack, we'll need them tonight.'

Jack piled the rugs in his arms. Peggy took the kettle and the saucepan. They went back to the outer cave, and then looked for the others outside. Mike had got a good fire going. Paul was sitting beside it in delight. He had never seen a campfire before.

'Nora, get the cocoa tin, a bag of sugar, and the tinned milk,' said Peggy. 'Mike, go to the spring and fill this kettle with water, will you? I'll boil water for the cocoa and we'll add milk and sugar afterwards.'

Mike went off with the kettle to the cold spring that gushed out from the hillside and ran down it in a little stream. He soon filled it and came back. 'What are we going to have to eat?' he asked hungrily.

'Soup out of a tin, bread, biscuits, and cocoa,' said Peggy.

'Ooooooh!' said everyone in delight. Mike opened the tin, glad that Dimmy had remembered to put in a tin-opener! He poured the rich tomato soup into the saucepan, and then set it on the fire firmly. 'Shall I make another fire to boil the kettle?' he asked.

'Oh no,' said Peggy. 'The soup will soon be ready, and we've got to cut the bread, and get out the biscuits. You do that, Nora. Where's the biscuit tin, Mike?'

The soup cooked in the saucepan. Peggy sent Jack for cups and dishes and bowls and spoons from the inner cave. The kettle was put on to boil. Peggy cleverly poured the soup from the saucepan into the dishes and handed a plateful to everyone. Hunks of bread were given out too. The kettle sang on the fire, and the smoke rose in the moonlight and floated away in the clear air.

'This is simply perfect,' said Mike, tasting his tomato soup and putting big pieces of bread into it. 'I wish this meal could last for ever.'

'You'd get pretty tired of tomato soup if it did!' said Jack. Everyone laughed. Peggy made the cocoa and handed round big cups of it, with tinned milk and sugar, and a handful of biscuits for everyone.

How they enjoyed that meal by the camp-fire! Mike said he wished they needn't go to sleep – but they were all so terribly sleepy that it was no good wishing that!

'I shall fall asleep sitting here soon,' said Nora, rubbing her eyes. 'What a nice supper that was! Come on, everyone, let's make our beds in the heather and wash the supper things tomorrow.'

So they spread the rugs out in the soft heather and lay down just as they were in their clothes – and in two seconds they were all fast asleep on the secret island, lost in happy dreams of all they were going to do the next day!

# Peace on the Island

All night long the five children slept soundly on their rugs in the heather. The three boys were in the shelter of a big gorse bush, and the two girls cuddled together beside a great blackberry bush. The heather was thick and soft and as springy as any bed.

The sun rose up and the sky became golden. The birds twittered and two yellowhammers told everyone that they wanted a 'little bit of bread and *no* cheese!' The rabbits who had played about near the sleeping children shot off to their holes. A rambling hedgehog sniffed at Mike, and then went away too.

Jack awoke first. He was lying on his back, and he was very much astonished when he opened his eyes and looked straight up into the blue sky. He had expected to see the ceiling of his bedroom at Peep-Hole – and he saw sky and tiny white feathery clouds, very high up.

Then he remembered. Of course – they were on the dear old secret island! He lay there on his back looking up happily at the sky, waiting for the others to wake. Then he sat up. Far below him were the calm, blue waters of the lake. It was a perfect day – sunny, warm, and calm. Jack looked at his watch, and stared in surprise – for it was half-past nine!

'Half-past nine!' said Jack in amazement. 'How we

have slept! I wish the others would wake up – I'm jolly hungry.'

He got up cautiously and slipped his few clothes off. He ran down to bathe in the lake. The water was delicious. He dried himself in the hot sun and dressed again. He went to the spring and filled the kettle for breakfast. Then he busied himself in making a fire.

Mike awoke next, and then Peggy and Nora together. Paul still slept on. The girls were full of joy to find themselves on the secret island, and they flew down to bathe in the lake with Mike. When Paul awoke they asked him if he too would like to have a swim, but he shook his head.

'I can't swim,' he said. 'And I don't want to bathe in the lake. I just want to stay here with Jack.'

They got breakfast. Nora ran down to the lake to wash the supper things. Jack fetched more wood for the fire, which was burning well. Peggy cut big slices of bread and butter, and popped some eggs into the saucepan to boil. 'Two eggs for everyone,' she said. 'I know quite well you'll all be able to eat heaps and heaps! Nora, find the salt, will you? I'll boil the eggs hard, and we can nibble them and dip them in the salt.'

'Let's have some of these ripe plums too,' said Mike, uncovering the basket. 'They won't last very long in this hot weather. And where are the biscuits, Peggy? Surely we didn't finish them all last night.'

'Of course not,' said Peggy, fishing them out from under a bush and taking off the lid. 'I hid them there because I know what you boys are like with biscuits!'

They sat round in the heather, eating their hard-boiled eggs, thick slices of bread and butter, ripe plums, and biscuits, and drinking cocoa that Peggy had made for them.

'I don't know why, but we always seem to have the most delicious meals on our secret island,' said Mike. 'They always taste nicer here than they do anywhere else.'

'Paul, don't you want your second egg?' asked Peggy, seeing that Paul had not eaten it. He shook his head.

'I am not used to your English breakfasts,' he said. 'At home, in my own country, we simply have a roll of bread and some coffee. But I would like to eat my egg later in the morning, Peggy. It is so nice. I have never had a hard-boiled egg before.'

Paul began to talk of his own land. He was a nice boy, with beautiful manners that struck the others as rather comic sometimes. He would keep bowing to Peggy and Nora whenever he spoke to them. He had learnt English from his governess, and spoke it just as well as the other children did.

He told them about his father and mother. He cried when he spoke of his mother, who did not know where he was. Peggy and Nora felt very sorry for the little prince. They comforted him, and told him that soon his troubles would be over.

'You are so lucky not to have to be princes or princesses,' he told the children. 'You can have a jolly time and do as you like – but maybe it will happen to me again sometime or other. There are many people who do not want me to be king when my father dies.'

'Do you want to be?' asked Jack.

'Not at all,' said Paul. 'I would like best of all to live

with you four children, and be an ordinary boy. But I am unlucky enough to have been born a prince and I must do my duty.'

'Well, stop worrying about things for a little while,' said Peggy. 'Enjoy your few days here on our secret island. It will be a real holiday for you. Jack will teach you to swim, and Mike will teach you how to make a campfire. You never know when things like that will be useful to you.'

The children all felt rather lazy after their late night. Peggy and Nora washed up the breakfast things, and Peggy planned the lunch. The children had eaten all the ripe plums and Peggy wondered if she should open a large tin of fruit. She would cook some potatoes and peas too, and they could have some of the meat off the cold joint they had brought.

'What about picking some wild raspberries, as we used to do last year?' asked Nora eagerly. 'Don't you remember the raspberry canes on one part of the island, Peggy? – they were simply red with delicious raspberries!'

'We'll go and see if there are any still ripe,' said Peggy. 'But first let's see if Willow House is still in the little wood beyond the beach.'

The children had built a fine little house of willow branches the summer before, which had sheltered them well on wet or cold days and nights. They all went running down the hill to see if Willow House was still standing.

They squeezed through the thick trees until they came to the spot where Willow House was – and it stood there, green and cool, inviting them to go inside.

'But the whole of Willow House is growing!' cried

Peggy. 'Every branch has put out leaves – and look at these twigs shooting up from the roof! It's a house that's alive!'

She was right. Every willow stick they had used to build their house had shot out buds and leaves and twigs – and the house was, as Peggy said, quite alive. Inside the house long twigs hung down like green curtains.

'Dear little Willow House,' said Peggy softly. 'What fun we had here! And how we loved making it – weaving the willow twigs in and out to make the walls – and you made the door, Jack. And do you remember how we stuffed up the cracks with heather and bracken?'

The others remembered quite well. They told Paul all about it and he at once wanted to stop and build another house.

'No, we don't need one,' said Jack. 'We can sleep out-of-doors now – and if rain comes we'll just sleep in the cave.'

Paul ran in and out of Willow House. He thought it was the nicest place in the world. 'I wish I had a house

of my own like this,' he said. 'Mike, Jack, will you come back to my country with me and teach me how to build a willow house?'

The boys laughed. 'Come along and see if we can find some ripe raspberries,' said Mike. 'You'll like those, Paul.'

They all went to the part of the island where the raspberries grew. There were still plenty on the canes, though they were nearly over now.

Peggy and Nora had brought baskets. Soon they had the baskets half-full, and their mouths were stained with pink. As many went into their mouths as into the baskets!

'It's one o'clock,' said Mike, looking at his watch. 'Good gracious! How the morning has gone!'

'We'll go back and have dinner,' said Peggy. So back they all went in the hot sun, feeling as hungry as hunters,

although they had eaten so many raspberries!

They had a lovely dinner – cold mutton, peas, potatoes, raspberries, and tinned milk. Mike brought them icy-cold water from the spring, and they drank it thirstily, sending Paul for some more when it was finished. Paul wanted to do jobs too, and Peggy thought it was a good idea to let him. The sun had caught his pale little face that morning and he was quite brown.

'What shall we do this afternoon?' asked Paul.

'I feel sleepy,' said Peggy, yawning. 'Let's have a nice snooze on the heather – then we could have a bathe before tea, and a jolly good meal afterwards.'

It was a lovely lazy day they had, and they thoroughly enjoyed it after all the alarms and adventures of the last week or two. Jack began to teach Paul to swim, but he was not very good at learning, though he tried hard enough!

They had tea, and then they went boating on the lake in the cool of the evening. 'We might try a bit of fishing tomorrow,' said Jack. 'It would be fun to have fried fish again, Peggy, just as we did last year.'

'Do you suppose we are quite, quite safe here?' asked Paul anxiously, looking over the waters of the lake as they rowed about.

'Of course!' said Jack. 'You needn't worry, Paul. Nobody will come to look for you here.'

'If Mr Diaz knew about your secret island he might come here to seek me,' said Paul. 'Hadn't we better keep a watch in case he does?'

'Oh no,' said Jack. 'There's no need to do that, Paul. Nobody would ever find us here, I tell you.'

'Where did you used to watch, when you were here last year and were afraid of people coming to look for you?' asked Paul.

'There's a stone up on the top of the hill where we used to sit, among the heather,' said Jack. 'You get a good view all up and down the lake from there.'

'Then tomorrow I will sit and watch there,' said Paul at once. 'You do not know Mr Diaz as well as I do, and I think he is clever enough to follow us, and to take me prisoner again. If I see him coming in a boat, there will be time to hide away in the caves, won't there?'

'Oh yes,' said Jack. 'But he won't come. Nobody will guess you are here with us.'

But Paul was nervous – and when the next day came he ran off by himself. 'Where's he gone?' asked Jack.

'Oh, up to the hill-top to watch for his enemies!' said Nora, with a laugh. 'He won't see anything. I'm sure of that!'

But Prince Paul *did* see something that very afternoon!

# The Enemy Find the Island

Prince Paul was sitting on top of the little hill that rose in the middle of the island. He was quite sure that his enemies would try to find him, and would think of coming to the children's secret island.

He sat there for two or three hours, watching the lake around the island. It was very calm and blue. Paul yawned. It was rather boring sitting there by himself – but the other children wouldn't come, for they said there was no fear of enemies coming so soon.

Paul saw Mike and Jack far below at the edge of the water. They were getting out the boat to go and fish. The girls came running down to join them. They had already asked Paul to come, but he wouldn't. He was really afraid of water, and it was all that the others could do to get him in to bathe.

Paul stood up and waved to the others. They waved back. They didn't like leaving him alone, but really they couldn't go and sit up there for hours. Besides, Peggy had said that if they caught some fish she would fry them for supper, and that really sounded rather delicious!

'We shan't be long, Paul!' shouted Mike. 'We shall only be round the south end of the island, which is a good fishing place. Yell to us if you want us.'

'Right!' shouted back Paul, and he waved again. He

really thought it was odd the way the four children seemed to like the water so much – they were always bathing and paddling and boating! But Paul liked them immensely, especially Mike, who had been a great help to him when he had been a prisoner in the tower.

He watched the boat leave the little beach and row round to the other side of the island. The boat looked very small from where he stood, and the children looked like dolls! But he could hear their voices very clearly. They were getting their fishing lines ready.

Paul half wished he was with them, they all sounded so jolly. He watched them for some time, and then he turned round and gazed down the blue waters of the lake on the other side of the island.

And he saw a boat there! Yes – a boat that was being rowed by two men! Paul stood and watched, his heart beating fast. Who were the two men? Could they be Mr Diaz and Luiz? He hated them both and was afraid of them. Had they come to find him again?

He turned to the opposite side of the lake and yelled to the four children in the boat there.

'Jack! Mike! There's a boat coming up the lake!'

'What?' shouted Jack.

Paul yelled again, even more loudly. 'I said, *there's a boat coming up the lake*!'

The four children looked at one another in dismay and surprise. 'Surely Mr Diaz can't have found out where we are,' said Mike. 'Though he's quite clever enough to guess, if he knows we are the children who ran away to a secret island last year!'

'What shall we do, Jack?' asked Nora.

'We haven't time to do anything much,' said Jack
anxiously. 'I think it wouldn't be safe to go and hide on
the island – those men will search it throughly, caves
and all. We'd better get Paul down here, and row off to
the mainland in the boat. We could hide in the trees
there for a bit.'

'Good idea, Jack,' said Mike. He stood up in the boat
and yelled to Paul, who was anxiously waiting for his
orders.

'Come on down here, Paul. We'll go off in the boat.
Hurry up!'

Paul waved his hand and disappeared. When he
appeared at the edge of the water, the others saw that he
was carrying something. He had a loaf of bread, a packet
of biscuits, and two tins of fruit!

'I say! You've got brains to think of those!' said Jack,
pleased. 'Good for you, Paul!'

Paul went red with pleasure. He thought the four
children were wonderful, and he was very proud to be
praised by Captain Jack!

'I just had time to push all our things into a bush,' said
Paul. 'And I grabbed these to bring, because I guessed

we might have to stop away for some hours.'

'Good lad,' said Jack. 'Come on in. We haven't any time to lose. Tell us about the boat. How far away was it?'

As Jack and Mike rowed their boat away from the island, away to the mainland, Paul told them all he had seen, which wasn't very much. 'I couldn't see who the men were, but they *looked* as if they might be Mr Diaz and Luiz,' he said. 'Oh, Jack – I don't want to be caught and kept a prisoner again. It is so lovely being with you.'

'Don't you worry,' said Jack, pulling hard at the oars. 'We'll look after you all right, if we have to stuff you down a rabbit hole and pile bracken over it to hide you!'

That made them all laugh, and Paul felt better. The boys were pulling across to the mainland swiftly, hoping to reach it before the other boat could possibly catch any sight of them. The island was between them and the strange boat, but it might happen that the two men rowed round it and would then see the children's boat.

They reached the mainland safely. Jack chose a very wooded part, and rowed the boat in right under some overhanging trees, where it could not possibly be seen. Then he and the others got out.

'I'd better climb a high tree and see if I can possibly see what's going on on the island opposite us,' said Jack.

'I'll climb one too,' said Mike. 'I'd like to watch as well. Come on, Paul, would you like to climb one too?'

'No, thank you,' said Paul, who didn't like climbing trees any more than he liked bathing.

'Well, you stay behind and look after the girls,' said Jack. Paul was pleased with that. It made him feel important.

But the girls didn't want looking after! They wanted to climb trees too! However, they busied themselves in looking for a clear space to picnic in.

Jack's tree was a very high one. He could see the island quite well from it. He suddenly saw the boat coming round one side of the island, and he knew who the two men were!

'Yes – it's our dear friend Mr Diaz and his sleepy helper Luiz,' thought Jack to himself. 'They must have missed seeing the little beach where we usually land, and they've come round to the other side of the island. Well, that means we can keep a jolly good watch on them!'

Mike and Jack watched the boat from their perches up in the trees. The two men landed and pulled the boat on to the shore. They stood and talked for a while and then they separated and went off round the island.

'I'm afraid they won't find us!' Jack called softly to Mike, who was at the top of a tree nearby. 'And unless they find the things we brought with us, that Paul so cleverly stuffed into a bush, they may not even think we've *been* to the island!'

'It was a good idea of yours to come across to the mainland, Jack,' answered Mike. 'We're safe enough here. We could even make our way through the woods and walk to the nearest town, if we had to!'

'Look! There's one of the men at the top of the hill,' said Jack. Mike looked. The hill was not near enough to see if the man was Mr Diaz or Luiz, but it was certainly one of them. He was shading his eyes and looking all down the waters of the lake.

'Good thing our boat's hidden!' said Mike. 'I wonder how long they're going to hunt round the island! I don't want to spend the night in these woods – there's no heather here and the ground looks very damp.'

The boys watched for two hours and then they began to feel very hungry. Mike left Jack on watch and climbed down to the girls, who had been picking a crop of wild strawberries, small and very sweet. Paul was with them, and he ran to Mike and rained questions on him about the men in the boat.

Mike told him all he had seen. 'But what I really came down for was to say we'd better have something to eat,' he said. 'I'll clean the fish we've caught, Peggy, and

light you a small fire. You can cook them, then, on some
hot stones, and we'll have a meal.'

He cleaned the fish they had caught, and made a fire.
'I hope the men on the island don't think our smoke is
anything to do with *us*!' he said.

They had a meal of cooked fish, bread, biscuits, and
wild strawberries. Then Mike went up his tree again
to watch, and Jack came down and had his share of the
meal. It was really rather fun. The children enjoyed
their dinner, and wished there was more of it!

'But we must keep the two tins of fruit, and the rest
of the bread and biscuits for later on in the day,' said
Peggy, putting them safely aside under a bush. 'Thank
goodness Paul had the brains to bring what he could!
We'd only have had the fish to eat if he hadn't!'

Jack and Mike took it in turns to watch from a tree
the rest of the day. They saw no more signs of the two
men on the island, but they knew that they had not left,
because their boat was still there.

When it began to get dark, and the boys could no
longer see clearly from their perches in the trees, Jack
wondered what was the best thing to do.

He climbed down and talked to the others. 'We'd
better have another meal,' he said, 'and finish the
rest of the food. I'm afraid we shall have to spend the
night here.'

'We could sleep in the boat,' said Nora. 'That would
be more comfortable than the damp ground here. There
are two old rugs in the boat too. And Peggy and I have
explored a bit and found where a great mass of bracken
grows. We could collect it before it's quite dark, and use

that for bedding in the boat! It will be fairly soft for us.'

'Good,' said Jack. 'Show us where the bracken is, Nora, and Paul, Mike, and I will carry armfuls to the boat. Peggy, will you get a meal?'

'Right,' said Peggy. It was dark to get a meal under the trees, but the little girl did the best she could. She opened the tins of fruit – Paul even had been sensible enough to snatch up the tin-opener! She cut the rest of the bread into slices, and put two biscuits for every one. That was all there was.

The boys and Nora came back with armfuls of bracken. They set it in the boat. Then they went back to where Peggy was waiting. Jack had his torch in his pocket, so they were able to see what they were eating. They shared the fruit in the tins, ate their bread and biscuits, and drank the fruit juice, for they were very thirsty.

'And now to bed,' said Jack. 'Bed in a boat! What strange adventures we have! But all the same, it's great fun!'

# Mike's Marvellous Idea

The children made their way to where the boat was tied to a tree. It was now piled with sweet-smelling bracken. Jack had taken up the seats, so that the whole of the boat was a bed. The two girls got in and cuddled down, and then the three boys settled themselves too. It was a bit of a squeeze, but nobody minded. They wrapped the two old rugs round them and talked quietly.

The lake-water lapped gently against the boat, saying 'lip-lip-lip' all the time. It was a pleasant sound to hear. An owl hooted in a trembling voice not far off. 'Ooooooooo! Oo-oo-oo-oo!'

Paul sat up in a fright. 'Who's that?' he said.

Mike pulled him down. 'It's only a bird called an owl, silly!' he said. 'Don't sit up suddenly like that, Paul, you pull the rug off us.'

Paul lay down again and cuddled up to the other two boys. He was glad that the noise was only made by a bird.

The moon came up soon, and shone down through the black branches of the trees above. The water of the lake turned to silver. 'Lip-lip-lip' it said all the time against the boat. Nora listened to it and fell asleep. Peggy lay on her back and looked at a star that shone through the trees, and suddenly fell asleep too. Paul was soon asleep, but Mike and Jack talked quietly for some time.

They couldn't imagine what Mr Diaz and Luiz were going to do next. If they stayed long on the island the children couldn't go back there – and as they had no food, this was serious. On the other hand, if they tried to make their way through the thick woods nearby, they might get quite lost.

'If only we could make Mr Diaz and Luiz prisoners, just as they made you and Paul, it would be grand,' said Jack. 'Then we could do what we liked.'

Mike lay silent for a moment – then he made such a peculiar noise that he really frightened Jack.

'Mike! What's up?' said Jack in alarm. 'Are you ill?'

'No,' said Mike in a very excited voice. 'It was only that I suddenly got such a marvellous idea I wanted to shout – and I only just stopped the shout in time. That was the funny noise you heard – me stopping the shout. But oh, Jack, I've really got the most *wonderful* idea!'

'What is it?' asked Jack in surprise.

'Well, it was you saying that you wished we could make Mr Diaz and Luiz prisoners that really gave me the idea,' said Mike. 'I know how we could! If we could only get their boat away from the island tonight, they wouldn't be able to leave – and they'd be prisoners there!'

'Mike! That's a most *marvellous* idea!' said Jack. 'It solves all our difficulties. You really are a clever chap! Once they are prisoners on the island, we can row to the village at the end of the lake, get a car, and go back to Peep-Hole in safety!'

'Yes,' said Mike, trembling with excitement. 'How shall we do it, Jack?'

'Wait a minute,' said Jack, frowning in the moonlight. 'I've just thought of something. Suppose Mr Diaz and Luiz can swim? They could easily swim across to the mainland and escape that way.'

'But they *can't* swim,' said Mike. 'I heard Luiz tell Mr Diaz he couldn't, and Mr Diaz said he couldn't either. It was when I was a prisoner up in the tower – they often used to come and sit with us there, and they talked to one another. So if neither of them can swim they really *would* be prisoners!'

Jack was so delighted that he wanted to sing and dance. He carefully took off his share of the rug and put it over the sleeping Paul.

'We needn't wake Paul or the girls,' he said. 'We will undress, Mike, then slip into the water over the edge of the boat, and swim to the island. You can swim as far as that, can't you?'

'Easily,' said Mike. 'Then we'll undo their boat, get into it and row off! Oh, Jack, this is the most exciting thing we've ever done! I wonder if they'll see us!'

'I don't expect so,' said Jack. 'They'll be asleep in our cave, I expect!'

The boys undressed without waking the girls or Paul.

They slid into the water over the side of the boat and swam off in the moonlit lake, only their two dark heads showing on the calm, silvery surface.

It was rather farther to the island than they expected. Mike was tired when they reached the men's boat, but Jack, who was a marvellous swimmer, was quite fresh. He got in and pulled Mike in too. He undid the rope that tied the boat to a tree.

Then he pushed off, the oars making a splashing noise in the silence of the night. No sooner had they gone a little way out on the lake than a shout came from the island, and Luiz stood up. He had been asleep on some heather, and had awakened to hear the sound of oars.

'Hey! That's our boat you've got! Bring it back at once!'

'We'll bring it back some day!' yelled back Jack in delight.

'You just bring it back now, at once!' yelled Luiz, suddenly realising that he and Mr Diaz would not be able to leave the island at all without a boat. 'You wicked boys!'

'Goodbye, dear friends,' shouted Jack, seeing Mr Diaz suddenly appearing down the hill. He had been sleeping in the cave and had awakened at the noise of shouting. 'See you some day soon!'

The two men were quite helpless. They could neither of them swim, they had no boat – they could do nothing but shout angrily, and that was no good at all! The boys simply laughed and waved to them.

When they reached their own boat, feeling rather cold and shivery, for they had no clothes on, they found the girls and Paul wide awake and rather scared. Peggy threw the boys their clothes, and called out to know where they had been and what all the noise was and where they had got the other boat.

'Can't you guess!' cried Nora. 'They've taken the enemies' boat – and now they are prisoners on our secret island, hurrah! Oh, Jack, what a marvellous idea! We were so scared when we woke up and found you two gone – but we might have guessed you were off on some wonderful idea!'

'It's Mike's idea,' said Jack, dressing quickly. 'It's one of the best ideas he's ever had! It worked beautifully too – Mr Diaz and Luiz are as angry as can be, but they can't do anything about it! As soon as it's light we'll row to the village at the end of the lake, get a car, and go off to Peep-Hole to see what Dimmy and George have done – and Mr Diaz and Luiz can have a nice little holiday on the island!'

Everybody laughed. They felt sure they would never be able to go to sleep again that night, but after a while they began to yawn – and before the moon had begun to slide down the sky they were all fast asleep once more, with Mr Diaz's boat tied safely alongside their own.

They woke when the stars had gone and the moon had slipped away. The sun was coming up in the east and the lake looked peaceful and blue. Not a cloud was in the sky.

'Goodness, I *am* hungry!' said Peggy. 'And we haven't got a single thing to eat!'

Mike grinned. He put his hand into his pocket and brought out a large packet of chocolate!

'I kept this till this morning, thinking it would come in very useful!' he said. 'We'll share it, and then we'll have to wait till we get to the village at the end of the lake for breakfast.'

'Good old Mike!' said everyone, delighted to see the chocolate. It had nuts in it and was most delicious. They sat in the early morning sunshine, munching it and giggling whenever they thought of Mr Diaz and Luiz!

'There they are, at the edge of the lake, trying to see us!' said Peggy. 'Well, they'll see us soon enough when we row out! What shall we do with their boat, Jack?'

'We'll leave it tied up here,' said Jack. 'It will be safe enough.'

So they left the extra boat behind, untied theirs, and rowed out on to the lake. Mr Diaz and Luiz saw them at once, and shouted, but the children took no notice at all. They rowed steadily away from the island down to the village at the end of the lake.

When they got there they tied up the boat and stepped out on to the sandy shore. They made their way to the village and soon came to a baker's shop. They bought warm new bread and some jam tarts. They went to the grocer's and bought half a pound of butter, some potted meat to spread on their bread, and some biscuits and chocolate. They also bought some ginger beer, and then sat down by the roadside to eat a peculiar, but very delicious breakfast!

Jack and Mike lent their pocket knives to everyone to spread the potted meat and butter on thick slices cut from the new loaf. How lovely it tasted!

Then they ate the jam tarts and the biscuits, munched the chocolate, and drank the ginger beer. They felt much better after their meal, and Jack looked about for a garage.

There wasn't one – but at that moment a bus rattled up and stopped nearby. The children went to ask if there was any bus that would take them near Spiggy Holes.

'My bus starts off again in ten minutes' time,' said the driver. 'I go as far as Cliftonside, and you can get a bus there to Spiggy Holes.'

The children were pleased. They got into the bus and waited for it to start. It set off at last and rumbled down the country lanes for an hour until it arrived at Cliftonside. Out tumbled the children, and they went to get the bus for Spiggy Holes. It didn't start for half an hour, so they went to buy some more ginger beer, for it was a hot day and they felt very thirsty again.

They arrived at Spiggy Holes at half-past twelve. The bus stopped a mile away from Peep-Hole and the children took a short cut across the fields.

'We'd better just keep a watch out in case anyone else is looking for Paul,' said Jack. 'You never know!'

So they kept a lookout, and walked beside the tall hedges to hide themselves till they got to Peep-Hole.

And what a surprise they had when they got to the field opposite Peep-Hole – for there on the grass was an aeroplane! It was painted a bright blue, and had silvery edges that shone in the sun!

The children stopped in the greatest surprise. Nobody was in the aeroplane. Nobody was about at all. They didn't know whether to go to Peep-Hole or not – did the aeroplane belong to the enemy? Or was it a friend's? It was all very mysterious indeed.

# Alone at Peep-Hole

The five children stared and stared at the aeroplane. Paul went rather pale.

'It looks like an aeroplane from my own country,' he said. 'Do you think my enemies have flown over here to find me? If only I knew what had happened to my father – whether he got better or not! I am very unhappy.'

'Cheer up, old son,' said Jack. 'We'll soon find out everything. I expect Dimmy has told the police to find out what's been going on in your country, and she'll tell us as soon as we find her.'

'I want to see Dimmy,' said Nora. 'I feel safe when I'm with her.'

'Well, let's go quietly to Peep-Hole without being seen, and find her,' said Mike. So they crept along by the tall hedge, turned into the little lane where Peep-Hole stood, and ran into the small front garden.

The front door was shut. It usually stood wide open. They went round to the back door. That was shut and locked too! The children stared at one another in surprise.

'Has Dimmy locked herself in?' they wondered. 'What's been happening?'

'All the ground-floor windows are shut too,' said Jack, who had been round looking. 'But there's one open up there – do you see it? I believe if I climb up that old pear tree there, I could wriggle along that branch and get on to the windowsill.'

'Well, be careful then,' said Peggy. 'It doesn't look very safe to me!'

Jack climbed the tree, hoisted up by Mike. He wriggled carefully along the big branch that waved near the window. The other children stood below and watched him – but a shower of little hard pears fell on their heads and they went back a few steps, laughing.

Jack got safely to the windowsill. He opened the window and jumped inside. They heard his footsteps pattering down the stairs.

Then the bolts were shot back, the key was turned, and Jack opened the door. 'Come on in,' he said. 'We'll just see if Dimmy is anywhere here – but there's not a sound in the house.'

The children hunted everywhere for Dimmy. She was gone. The house was quiet and lonely, and the children didn't know what to do. When would Dimmy come back? Where had she gone? Where was George? Perhaps they could find *him*.

'Well, I vote we have something to eat,' said Jack at last. 'There's some ham in the larder – I've just looked – and some tomatoes too and stale bread. We can pick plums from the garden as well. Come on!'

Over the meal the children talked about what they should do. Should they stay at Peep-Hole till Dimmy came back? But suppose she didn't come back! They didn't feel very safe at Peep-Hole, so near the Old House, without Dimmy or George, because perhaps somebody might find out they were there and come to catch poor

Paul again.

'Well, I don't think anyone has seen us come,' said Jack. 'And we won't light a fire, so nobody will see smoke from our chimney. We won't have any lights on tonight, either. We'll all sleep together in the top room of the tower, and lock the door and pile furniture against it. Then we'll be safe!'

'Things are getting a bit too exciting again,' said Nora, who was really beginning to long for a little peace. 'I wish Mr Diaz hadn't discovered our secret island – we should have been so happy and peaceful there. I don't like Peep-Hole without Dimmy.'

'I'll slip out down to the beach and see if George is anywhere about,' said Jack, thinking hard. 'If he is he'll come back with me, I'm sure – and he could tell me what's happened to Dimmy – and *I* could tell *him* what has happened to Mr Diaz and Luiz!'

The others laughed. They liked to think of Mr Diaz and Luiz, prisoners on the secret island, not knowing when they were to be taken off!

Jack slipped out of the back door and the others bolted it after him. They decided to keep watch from the windows, to see if anyone came near. So Peggy and Paul kept a watch from the front windows, and Mike and Nora from the back. But nobody came near. Not even a dog barked anywhere. It was all very still and peaceful.

The children talked to one another. Peggy found her knitting, and knitted and chatted to Paul. Mike did a jigsaw puzzle with Nora, looking up every other minute to make sure that nobody was coming in through the back garden.

A loud thumping on the back door startled everybody dreadfully. Mike jumped and dropped the jigsaw on the floor. He had seen nobody come into the back garden. Paul and Peggy ran in from the front room, looking quite scared.

'Who do you suppose it is?' whispered Nora.

'Can't imagine,' whispered back Mike. 'Anyway, we'd better all keep as quiet as possible, then maybe they'll go away.'

So they all kept very quiet. The thumping came again – somebody banging on the back door with his bare fists. 'Bang all you like,' said Mike in a low voice. 'You won't get in!'

'Let me in!' cried a voice – and how they all jumped with joy! For it was Jack's voice! It was he who was thumping on the door!

'What idiots we are!' cried Mike, leaping to his feet. 'We might have guessed it was Jack – but I never thought he'd be back so soon!'

They all tore downstairs to open the door to Jack. He came in, quite cross with them:

'Whatever did you keep me waiting all that time for?' he asked indignantly. 'I thought you must have gone to sleep!'

'Sorry, Jack,' grinned Mike. 'We didn't see you come, and we didn't expect you back so soon. We thought you might be the enemy. How did you get through the back garden without being seen?'

'Crawled under the currant bushes,' said Jack, with a grin. 'I thought I'd give you a surprise – but I seem to have given you a good fright instead.'

'Did you see George?' asked Mike eagerly.

'Not a sign of him,' answered Jack. 'His boat was there all right – but I couldn't see him anywhere on the beach, or in the fields either. *He* seems to have disappeared into thin air just like Dimmy!'

'It's all very peculiar,' said Mike. 'Where in the world has everybody gone – and why is that aeroplane there – and what's been happening whilst we were on our island?'

'I wish I could tell you,' said Jack. 'What about some tea, Peggy? Are there any cakes in the tin?'

Peggy and Nora boiled a kettle for tea, and cut some bread and butter. There was honey on the larder shelf, and some gingerbread in the cake tin. They ate it all, and wished there was more.

'I vote we take something up to the tower bedroom for supper, and go up there now,' said Mike, when they had finished. 'We can lock ourselves in, and be safe till morning. The two girls can have my bed, and we three boys can share Jack's bed and that old sofa. We shall sleep till the morning!'

'I feel jolly tired now,' said Nora. 'It's all the excitement, I expect. Let's take the snap cards up with us and have a game. I shall go to sleep unless I do something!'

So after they had washed up the tea things, Peggy collected some supper and Jack hunted for the snap cards. They saw that all the downstairs windows and doors were fastened, and then they went upstairs to the top bedroom of the tower. They locked the door and sat down to play snap.

Paul had never played snap before, and he was

dreadfully bad at it. He simply could *not* see when two cards were alike, and the others made him jump when they yelled out 'snap'.

'I can see why you call it snap!' he said at last. 'You snap at one another like dogs! It is a game for dogs, not children.'

That made the others roar with laughter. And it was whilst they were laughing that they heard a strange noise. They all looked up.

'An aeroplane!' said Jack. 'Is it that one in the field going away?'

They rushed to the window. No – the blue and silver plane was still there – but another plane was soaring

round and round, on the point of landing. Mike caught up the field glasses that lay on the windowsill, and looked at the aeroplane through them.

Then he gave such a tremendous yell that poor Paul fell off his chair and tumbled in a heap on the ground!

'Mike! What's up?' cried the others.

'It's Daddy's plane!' shouted Mike, dancing round in joy. 'Can't you see the red on it? I bet Daddy and Mummy have flown over from Ireland, because Dimmy is sure to have let them know about us and Prince Paul! Oh, if they're back everything's all right!'

The others screamed with delight, and hung out of the window to watch the plane. It circled down over the field, and came neatly to rest beside the blue and silver plane. The propellers stopped whizzing round. Two people climbed out of the cockpit, dressed in flying clothes.

'Come on! It's Dad and Mummy all right!' shouted Mike. He raced to the door and unlocked it. He tore down the stairs with all the others at his heels and unlocked and unbolted the front door. Then like a pack of dogs the children scampered over the lane, and across the big field to the aeroplanes.

'Children! We thought you were safely on the secret island!' cried their mother's voice. She took off her helmet and smiled at them all. They crowded round her and hugged her. Prince Paul held back shyly. But Mrs Arnold drew him to her and gave him a hug like the rest.

'Where's Dimmy?' said Captain Arnold. But nobody knew!

# The End of the Adventures

'Come on back to Peep-Hole, Dad,' said Mike. 'We'll tell you everything there!'

So they all went back to Peep-Hole, and, sitting in the front room, they talked at the tops of their voices. All that Captain and Mrs Arnold had heard was that the children had rescued somebody and taken him off to their secret island. Dimmy had sent them a long telegram because they had moved from place to place in Ireland, and she could not get hold of them to telephone the news.

Then they had tried to telephone Dimmy but had got no answer, so they had got into their aeroplane and flown straight over to Spiggy Holes to find out what was the matter.

'And here we are!' said Captain Arnold. 'What about some food? I'm famished! We've got a hamper in the plane – go and get it, Jack and Mike.'

The boys tore off to get it – but as they went across the lane to the field, they heard the sound of a big car coming down the road. They stopped and looked. Peep-Hole was at the end of the lane – the road stopped just there, so whoever came down the lane *must* go to Peep-Hole. Who was coming?

The car was full of men. There were at least five.

Mike caught hold of Jack's arm and they fled back to Peep-Hole. 'They might be coming to take Paul away!' he yelled. 'Quick, come back and we'll lock the doors. Thank goodness Dad and Mummy are there!'

They shot back into the house and locked the front door. The car stopped outside with a screech of brakes, and four men got out. They were all in some kind of uniform and looked rather grand. They walked up the path and thundered on the knocker.

'Who's that?' said Captain Arnold in astonishment.

'We don't know,' said Mike. 'But we've locked them out in case they've come for Paul.'

'My dear boy, nobody can take Paul now I'm here,' said Captain Arnold. 'Open the door.'

But somebody else opened the door. Paul had been looking out of the window – and he suddenly gave a most ear-piercing yell, shouted something in a foreign language, and tore to the front door. He struggled with the bolts, yelling all the time.

'He's gone mad!' said Jack in surprise. 'Here, let me help you, Paul, since you're determined to open the door!'

The door opened. Paul flew through it, flung himself at the front man, and wept tears all down his chest! The man stroked him and patted him, whilst every one looked on in the greatest astonishment.

The man put Paul down and bowed most politely to Captain and Mrs Arnold.

'I am Paul's father, the King of Baronia,' he said.

'But we thought you were very ill, and nearly dying!' cried Mike, in surprise.

'Yes, I have been ill, but now I am better, much to the grief of my enemies,' said the King, in a grim sort of voice. 'Paul was made prisoner and taken away whilst I lay ill, and we did not know where he was. Then your Miss Dimity informed your good English police, and they sent the message to me that you children had rescued my boy, and had taken him to your secret island.'

'Then is that blue and silver aeroplane yours?' cried Mike. 'Paul said he thought it belonged to his country.'

'Yes, we flew over in it, I and my four friends,' said the King. 'We came to see Miss Dimity, that brave and good woman, and she and your friend George told us all that had happened.'

'But where *is* Dimmy?' asked Nora, almost in tears, for she really felt very anxious about Dimmy.

'Miss Dimity is coming in another car,' said the king. 'She and George and ourselves all had to go to the police to explain what had happened. She will soon be here.'

And even as he spoke another car drew up outside, and out leapt George to help Miss Dimity. She got out, looking rather pale and tired, but just the same cheerful old Dimmy. She couldn't believe her eyes when the children rushed to greet her.

'I thought you were safely on your secret island!' she said. 'What made you leave it?'

'Oh, Dimmy, it's a long story!' said Mike. 'Come along in – look who's here!'

'Your father and mother!' said Dimmy, in amazement.

'So the second aeroplane is theirs, I suppose. Captain Arnold, I *am* glad to see you! I couldn't seem to find out *where* you were in Ireland. What a meeting this is – Paul's father and friends, and you too, and the children!'

The little front room was too small to hold them all, so they went into the garden. George brought out seats for everybody, and it was a very noisy party that sat out there and talked and talked.

'If only I could get my hands on Diaz and Luiz, the traitors!' said Paul's father angrily, as Paul told him how he had been kept prisoner.

'Well, you can if you want to,' said Mike, with a grin. 'We've made *them* prisoners now! You can catch them as soon as you please!'

'Where are they then?' cried Dimmy.

'On our secret island without a boat!' laughed Mike. 'And there they'll stay till somebody goes over and catches *them*!'

Everybody laughed in delight. It was very funny to think of the two bad men being caught like that.

'Tomorrow morning I and the policemen will go over in a boat,' said the King grimly. 'Diaz and Luiz will be *most* surprised to see us! They meant to prevent my son Paul from being king after me if I died – and now that I am very much alive, they will be sorry they ever thought of such a plan!'

'Will you take Paul back with you?' said Mike, feeling sorry that they were to lose a boy he liked very much.

'Yes,' said the King. 'But next term he is to come to school in your good, safe country of England, and maybe he could go to your school, Jack and Mike?'

'Oh, good!' said the two boys, pleased. 'We'll look after him!'

'I'm sure you will!' said Paul's father, clapping both boys on the back. 'You've looked after him marvellously so far!'

'Well, what are we all going to do tonight?' said Dimmy. 'I'd like to ask you all to stay with me, but Peep-Hole is too small! I could put Captain and Mrs Arnold into my spare room, but there's no other room, I'm afraid.'

'We shall go to the nearest town and stay at the hotel there,' said the King. 'Paul must go with us, for I feel I cannot let him out of my sight! Tomorrow we will come again, Miss Dimity. Thank you a thousand times for all you have done!'

The King and Prince Paul, and the four men in uniform said goodbye and went to their big car. It started up, and, with a terrific noise, shot up the lane.

'We've forgotten all about the hamper of food,' said Jack suddenly. 'Let's go and get it now, Mike. I feel as if I could eat my hat!'

'I'd like to see you!' said Mike. The two of them set off to the aeroplane. They climbed into the cockpit and found a larger hamper there. They carried it between them to Peep-Hole.

They all had a picnic in the garden – George too. How they enjoyed it! They told their stories again and again.

'Mr Diaz, Mrs Diaz, and Luiz all came to Peep-Hole in a furious rage the night you went to the secret island,' said Dimmy. 'Luckily by the time they got here, George was back, so between the two of us we sent them off. They were quite sure that the Prince was here with you.'

'They must have found out somehow about our island, and where it was,' said Mike. 'Well, it's a story that everybody knows, so that wouldn't have been very difficult. Oh, wouldn't I like to see the faces of those two on the island tomorrow, when the King and the police go to fetch them!'

And, indeed, Mr Diaz and Luiz did get a dreadful shock when a boat, full of English policemen, arrived at the secret island the next day! The two men were busy working at making a rough raft to paddle across to the mainland and they did not hear the boat arriving. They looked up from their work to see the King of Baronia walking towards them, with five men behind him!

The children heard all about it the next day. 'That finishes Mr Diaz and his plots,' said Jack, pleased. 'What a good thing we came to Spiggy Holes for our holidays! Young Paul would still have been a prisoner, and we wouldn't have had all these adventures.'

That evening George came running in, in a state of great excitement. 'Come and see,' he cried. 'Come and see!'

The children and Dimmy ran out into the road – and there, coming down the lane, drawn on an enormous trailer, was the finest little motorboat that anybody could wish for!

'It's coming to Peep-Hole!' cried Jack.

So it was! It was a present to the four children from the King of Baronia for all their help to his son. The children could hardly believe their eyes!

'What a wonderful present!' they cried. 'Oh, George, let's launch it this evening!'

It was impossible to get the motorboat down to the beach. It had to be taken to Longrigg and unshipped there. George's brother helped. It was launched on the calm, evening waters, and everyone got in, Dimmy too. It was so easy to drive that the children could take it in turns.

The motor started up with a lovely whirring sound. The little boat leapt forward. Mike swung her out to sea, feeling as proud as could be. A motorboat of their own! How lucky they were!

Now they're off, all the way back to Peep-Hole. Goodbye, Mike – goodbye, Jack! Goodbye, Nora and Peggy! You deserve your good luck, and we loved all your adventures. Maybe we'll hear more of them another day. Goodbye, goodbye!